The Omen
at
Rosings Park

How Elizabeth
Became Mrs. Darcy
A Pride and Prejudice Variation

Joseph P. Garland

DERMODY
HOUSE
PUBLISHING

DermodyHouse.com

The Cover:
Mrs. Klapp (Anna Milnor) and Dr. Joseph Klapp (1814), by Thomas Sully (American, 1783-1872) Courtesy of the Art Institute of Chicago
https://www.artic.edu/artworks/72375/mrs-klapp-anna-milnor

From the Institute:

"Thomas Sully's portrayal of Philadelphian Anna Milnor Klapp features her Empire-style dress and stand-up collar with flourishing brushstrokes of silver, gray, and white. The fluted, monumental column in the background underscores the period taste for elegance and classical traditions. The companion portrait depicts Joseph Klapp in contemplation, emphasizing his study of medicine. Together, the portraits present an image of a sophisticated couple that celebrates their prosperity, intelligence, and taste."

Contents

Introduction

This is a *Pride and Prejudice* Variation. Unlike my first novel related to that novel, *Becoming Catherine Bennet*, this novella makes a major alteration in the original. I have attempted to match the story until shortly after Mr. Collins proposes to Elizabeth Bennet. She still rejects him at first, but here she is, to use an Austenian, persuaded to (unlike Anne Eliot, that other great Austen heroine) to accept the hand offered to her.

Chapter 1. Elizabeth's Move to Hunsford

It rained, though it was not a heavy rain, on the afternoon of the Tuesday when Mrs. William Collins left Meryton (in Hertfordshire) to live at Hunsford (in Kent). The newly married Mr. and Mrs. hurried to the cover of the second-best of Lady Catherine de Bourgh's carriages, an older barouche she'd most graciously sent to collect her clergyman and the cousin he'd selected as his bride.

Elizabeth Collins—Elizabeth Bennet as was—had yet to see the Parsonage where she was soon to live nor the grand house that hovered near it. In some ways, though, from her new husband's descriptions, she almost believed that she had long resided in one and close to the other.

Elizabeth did not regret her decision to marry this near stranger and distant relation who she knew to be stupid and vain in about equal portions. What she did regret was its necessity. Her first reaction to his proposal was shock and surprise and, of course, rejection. But her mother took her own appeal that she *accept* him to her father and much as he, too, thought Mr. Collins a fool, the fact was that he, Mr. Bennet, had failed to provide for his daughters when he had the chance to do so. He was perhaps the bigger fool, and he convinced himself, or at least was resigned to the reality, that other men must be found to provide for his five daughters, even when fifteen years earlier he knew they'd be no Bennet son. Mr. Collins was there and available, so Mr. Bennet decided that the selfish clergyman was as adequate (financially if not in other respects) as any man for Lizzy. Indeed, he was the only one to have appeared and asked to take her on.

On that late autumn morning in 1811, while Mr. Collins paced some feet from Mrs. Bennet (and under the watchful eyes of Elizabeth's sisters from a pair of upstairs windows) near the shrubbery that bordered the garden to the front of the house, Mr. Bennet spoke to his second daughter. They were in his library. She sat stiffly near the front of one of the pair of intricate wooden armchairs he favoured when he wished to "speak in seriousness" with someone. He had sunk somewhat into the other.

"An unhappy alternative is before you, Elizabeth," he said, "for you may never have such an opportunity again and seeing as you are a clever girl—not nearly so silly as your sisters—and he is not a clever man, I believe you can make a fine life for yourself with some significant measure of security by accepting him."

"Oh, papa."

"I have long been pressed on by our reality. We cannot know if the recent attentions paid to Jane will be anything but a passing breeze. I will sleep better knowing that Longbourn will remain in our family when I am gone, and I hope knowing that will allow *you* to sleep better."

"Then you say I must accept him?"

"Lizzy, I do not know that you have a choice."

She stood and through the large window saw Mr. Collins and her mother speaking on the graveled walk, Mrs. Bennet the far more animated of the two.

"I'm sorry, Elizabeth. I truly am," her father told her from his chair.

"I understand, papa." She laughed with an effort. "I shall have him tend to the garden he speaks so highly of and tend, I imagine, to his patroness and her daughter most of the time. I should think I can make myself largely free of him and them to enjoy my books and my correspondence and perhaps"—and she touched her belly—"I will have a little boy to spoil."

With that, she was through the door.

Now on a lightly raining day nearly a month later, she had become Mrs. William Collins and was heading to that garden and that patroness and her daughter and she was very, very frightened.

As they rode south, she permitted her husband to clasp her hand while he extolled and re-extolled the wonders that awaited her. The house and the grounds. The widow and the daughter. The chimneys and the staircases. The life and the…

* * * *

IN THE MONTHS TO FOLLOW, Mrs. Collins did not come to share her husband's enthusiasm for some of these things—who could have?—and in fact developed a starkly different view, particularly as to the widow and the daughter. It was a blessing, then, that she spent relatively little time seeing either de Bourgh. Mr. and Mrs. Collins were invited to the great house but rarely. Miss de Bourgh occasionally stopped when she passed the Parsonage on the way to or from Hunsford but never accepted an invitation to enter the house or to leave her phaeton, even to explore the Parsonage's fine garden.

Mrs. Collins, though, found she could tolerate her own absence from Longbourn and her presence in Hunsford and especially her husband more easily with each passing day. His imperfections were substantial indeed, but she managed to direct his natural desire to make himself of service to the de Bourghs (and encourage him as to his parishioners). She also succeeded in encouraging his enthusiasm for tending to that fine garden, which extended along the northern side of the Parsonage and had a mix of flowers and vegetables.

In part, her husband's labour allowed her to enjoy the solitude she found on the inside of the house, of the small room on the first floor that was dedicated to her own use, with a fireplace, desk, and several comfortable chairs that allowed her to look out over that garden whilst she read novels (at her own insistence and notwithstanding her husband's disapproval) or wrote letters.

Mrs. Collins made it a point to travel in several circuits each week in the Parsonage's little gig-and-pony among the parishioners. She read widely and wrote often. As to her correspondence, it was a great disappointment if more than three or four days passed without receiving something, however pedestrian, in return.

Elizabeth was most dedicated and intimate with her older sister Jane and her best friend Charlotte. The former was chiefly at her aunt and uncle's house in the Cheapside area of London. The latter was married to Thomas Sebel, a good man and respected lawyer who had a small house in a town just ten miles east of Meryton.

Poor Jane, though, the eldest (and prettiest and sweetest) of the five sisters, had yet to find the person with whom she could be happy. It was something of a blessing that Elizabeth had married Mr. Collins. That provided some level of security for the other Bennet sisters and allowed Jane to be more particular about the one to whom she would eventually extend her affections. Yet again and again in her visits to her aunt and uncle in London, Jane Bennet found no eligible gentleman with whom she believed she could be comfortable and Elizabeth, alone among the Bennets, understood that Jane *had* known such a man. And Jane still struggled with the fact that he was lost to her forever, gone back to town from Netherfield, the estate but three miles from Longbourn, only days after Elizabeth's engagement. Jane, it seemed, preferred the life of a spinster loving and caring for her cousins (the four Gardiner children) and perhaps the nieces and nephews that her sisters would produce, and prayed that it might be enough for her.

Alas, Elizabeth had yet produced either of such offspring, a regret not particularly softened by her husband's insistence that it was God's way and not aided by Lady Catherine's insistence that it must be her fault that they'd failed to produce a baby Collins.

Chapter 2. The Colonel's Return from War

Colonel Richard Fitzwilliam could not be more pleased, hopping as he was from a hackney cab on Brook Street in the very superior Mayfair area of London. He leapt up three steps to the shiny ebony door with its gleaming brass "40" on it and pulled the bell. It was the house of his great friend and cousin, Fitzwilliam Darcy. He, the Colonel, had been released briefly from his regiment after it returned from an extended stay on the Iberian Peninsula. He did not know for how long he would remain in England and would make the most of it before he was again called upon to serve King and Country.

It was always a chancy thing, but his great hope was that he would find a woman of some fortune—forty- or fifty-thousand would do quite nicely—and a sweet enough disposition. And then he could retire happily and become a true gentleman, like his brother (the presumptive next earl) and, of course, like Darcy.

The door was quickly opened, and he was quickly being directed by the long-familiar Bradley, Darcy's butler, into the fine sitting room with its view to the street. He was not there long before his friend was embracing him and, in a moment, had separated himself from the officer—who was resplendent in his regimentals—and eyed him from head to toe before smiling.

"I see you are none the worse for wear, Fitzwilliam," said the host, to which his guest retorted with a "In contrast to you, Darcy, who has become frightfully old in my absence and, I will say, frightfully fat enjoying the protection of His Majesty's Army."

"Indeed," Darcy said. "And let us not forget the Navy."

"I suppose those vagabonds are entitled to some thanks since we are, after all, an island nation."

"You are too generous," Darcy replied as he stepped to a small table along the wall. There he lifted a decanter of claret and poured a fair portion of its contents into a pair of Irish crystal glasses. After returning the container to the table, he carried the two. He handed one to the Colonel.

"To the King," Darcy said as he lifted his glass just as Fitzwilliam was lifting his.

"To the King," was echoed, and the men each took a long drink from his glass. The host again lifted his wine. When Fitzwilliam had done the same, Darcy said, "And to God for seeing to the safe return of my precious cousin."

"To your most precious *male* cousin, I should think," said Fitzwilliam, which was echoed this time by Darcy, and they drank once more.

The final toast was to "our dear cousin Anne," and they each drained their glasses and restored them, empty, to the table.

"Have you become engaged to her, Darcy?" Fitzwilliam asked.

"I expect it will happen soon enough. Perhaps I will do so when we go down to Rosings later this month," Darcy said, "that being the primary reason for our going there instead of to Pemberley this year."

"I will say, Darcy, much as I believe Pemberley vastly superior to Lady Catherine's estate, it is so much more distant from town."

"Indeed, and it always does well for us to visit our aunt."

"Though," Fitzwilliam said, "more important for a penniless second son than for you, my dear cousin."

Whereupon the two settled deeply into the host's favourite pair of leather chairs and Darcy allowed the Colonel to regale him with tales of conquests and close shaves, on the battlefield and off, until Bradley returned with news that a light bit of refreshment had been set out in the dining parlour.

Chapter 3. Mr. Darcy's Regrets

"There was a girl, as I daresay there often is," Darcy told his cousin later that month. The officer and the gentleman were sitting very comfortably in the Rosings library that had been the late Sir Lewis de Bourgh's. The great house had in fact passed to their cousin Anne (though it was universally acknowledged as being Lady Catherine's). It sat majestically in the Kentish countryside.

The two had just finished dinner at the aunt's table and with the aunt's daughter. They were now alone and settled into their fat leather armchairs, each with a fine claret in superb French crystal, and their talk had drifted from what was clearly the wish of their aunt. That Darcy marry Anne de Bourgh.

"Tell me about this girl," the Colonel said as the pair were enjoying Lady Catherine's—in spirit Sir Lewis's—superb wine. Darcy rose and refilled his glass, lifting the decanter to his friend, who declined. He came back and resumed his seat, taking a long draught of the wine before lowering his glass and holding its stem between his fingers above his lap.

"My friend Charles Bingley—who you've met in town—was renting an estate in a quiet part of Hertfordshire. As is the custom in such country parts, a fuss was made about a local assembly commemorating some event or another. It would have been churlish for him not to attend and so he did, bringing not only his sisters but me as well."

He took a slight sip of his drink before placing the glass on a table beside his chair.

"You know my view of the country."

"Yes, Darcy, I've heard you say one moves in a very confined and unvarying society in a country neighbourhood. Other than, of course, around Pemberley."

"True enough," Darcy said with the sort of smile he reserved for his closest friends, of whom his cousin was one, "I may have said some such thing a time or two."

"The girl, Darcy. Tell me of this girl you mention."

"Word had reached us that there were some few women and girls of some accomplishment and much beauty and so I went to the country ball with great expectations as to who would be there."

"Even if they were mere country girls?"

"I was willing to be convinced."

"You, Darcy? Willing to table your prejudices on that front? I should have liked to have accompanied you."

Darcy ignored this slight.

"Charles and I rolled up with his sisters and his brother-in-law and, of course, much was made of our appearance. It was like some country livestock auction with mothers pressing their daughters to the front of the crowd and I was half-tempted to check the teeth on some of them as we passed."

"You are incorrigible, but I must know about this evasive girl."

"Ah, the girl. I was never, in fact, properly introduced to her but—" (he took a quiet sip) "she was, in fairness, far more a woman. She was there with her four sisters and, my God, how her mother was the very epitome of an ill-raised country mother. Daughter of a country lawyer, I believe."

"Who cares about the mother?"

"Indeed. There were five of them, daughters I mean. The oldest was very pretty, I will say that, but she lacked any sort of spirit or depth, though my friend found her enchanting."

"But you did not."

"It will take more than a pretty face to tempt me."

"But this other one, I'm guessing that she *did* tempt you."

"She was the second daughter. The other three were truly girls of no consequence. Two of them, one about Georgiana's age I think, flitted about like children and the other seemed to accept participating in the amusement as some type of dreary obligation."

Darcy reached for and lifted his glass, took yet another sip, and retained it between his fingers, turning it this way and that without conscious thought.

"At first I found the one of whom I speak tolerable and not handsome, though she'd been labeled a beauty."

Though his glass was still half full, he again rose for more wine. When he put the decanter back down after the Colonel had again declined a topping off, he turned to his cousin.

"I did not dance with any of the country girls."

"I've told you that you must make more of an effort at such events."

"Perhaps someday," said Darcy, still by the sideboard, "I will but I did not that evening and we left after Bingley engaged in dancing enough for the pair of us. Things got very peculiar after the ball. His sisters invited the girl's older sister—and *just* her older sister—to their house for a visit when Charles was out. But the sister fell ill from being caught in the rain and as a matter of kindness the sisters—Bingley's sisters—allowed her to stay until she was well enough to travel back to her own home. The sister, the one I'm referring to—"

"The one you won't get to."

"Indeed, the one I haven't got to. She appeared a day later, having walked the three miles from their home through the muck and the mud to see how her sister fared."

"She didn't have a carriage?"

"She was...peculiar, in an intriguing way such women can be. I spent a fair amount of time with her over the ensuing days. And like a fool I didn't fully understand her, though I was impressed by her devotion to her sister."

"Her name, Darcy? What is her name?"

"Didn't I say? Elizabeth. Elizabeth Bennet."

Darcy returned to his chair, cradling his wine.

"Over time, given what I took to be Charles's infatuation with the eldest Miss Bennet, I found myself in the presence of Miss Elizabeth with some frequency. I confess I was not as discreet as I might have been, though I daresay she never suspected a thing as to my growing fascination with her. With observation, I began to find her face was rendered uncommonly intelligent by the beautiful expression of her dark eyes."

"You are now a romantic, Darcy? I hardly know you."

"Indeed, I hardly know, or knew, myself. She was not in the least fashionable in her manners but had an easy playfulness one would never encounter in town."

"Especially by a single woman in want of a large fortune."

"Quite so. Especially not. She was lacking in perfection in any particular, but I now realise that she came together quite well. Her looks alone were light and pleasing."

"And the rest of her?"

"That is the worst part. Light and pleasing as she was in appearance, she was...intriguing in herself and I think had I given her a chance I would have found it very pleasing, if not light. I think I should have very much enjoyed going for walks with her and simply sitting of an evening with her nearby."

"Did you not pursue her? She was a gentleman's daughter, was she not?"

"She was. There were some difficulties in that regard, though. He had five daughters and no sons, and his estate was entailed."

"To whom?"

"To, much to my regret, a distant cousin."

"'Regret'?"

"The daughters had to marry well although the reality of their family situation and relations made that difficult. I understand now why their mother was so intent on that, more so than most mothers, I think. Were the father to die, they'd all be left in near poverty with only slight funds for themselves were none of them to marry well."

"Not unlike me, being a second son and needing himself to marry well for just that reason."

"The way of the world, Richard. The way of *our* world. You could at least have a colonel's commission purchased for you. And I'm afraid that's where that distant cousin comes in. He is, in fact, Mr. Collins."

"'Mr. Collins'? The parson?"

"The very same. The one given a living in Hunsford by Lady Catherine."

"So, he will inherit the Bennet estate?"

"He will inherit the Bennet estate. And at Lady Catherine's suggestion, he traveled to that estate some months ago and not long after I first encountered the Bennet family. His specific intent was to find one of the daughters to marry."

"Him? He seems such a stupid fellow."

"He is, but he has somehow earned the favour of Lady Catherine. In any case, he went to Longbourn—that's the Bennet estate—and proposed to Miss Elizabeth Bennet and she after some hesitation apparently said yes."

"But if she was as you say, why would she accept him?"

"Because what choice did she have? When her father dies, she will become mistress of Longbourn and be able to protect her mother and those of her sisters who remain at home."

"Now I see. If she is Mrs. Collins, I assume I will meet her presently."

"Yes. Lady Catherine informed me that they would be invited to dinner while we are here."

"And this is what brought back memories of her?"

Darcy took a sip, a larger sip, of his claret. "I'm afraid I cannot say that. For months it has taken very little, sometimes nothing at all, to bring back thoughts of that woman. She has long tortured me. Even in my sleep. I've long compared her to the women I meet, those who thrust themselves at me."

"Like Bingley's sister?"

"Especially like Caroline Bingley. And none of them was or is or, I'm afraid, ever could be her equal. In beauty or any other womanly trait."

"Since this Miss Elizabeth is now Mrs. Collins, I gather that you are finally resigned to marrying our cousin Anne."

"And joining the de Bourgh estate with Pemberley? It is what is expected and having lost the one opportunity to truly be content by my pride and refusal to see beyond her family, I believe, yes, that I am so resigned."

"Your prejudices have done you in, then, as I always feared they would."

"And I was too proud to do what I now regret more than I daresay anything in my life. Not giving her the slightest encouragement about my growing feelings towards her."

"And her sister? The beautiful one?"

"It is not my proudest moment and perhaps was beneath me, but I convinced Charles that there was not the slightest hint of true affection on the side of Miss Bennet. I said that she'd likely forgotten him before he'd reached town upon leaving the rented country house. So he was convinced, rightly I believe, of her indifference and nothing more was done about it or with her. I do not know what became of her and I'm sure that given her family—"

"Other than Miss Elizabeth."

"Indeed, other than Miss Elizabeth. They are quite inappropriate. It would have been a degradation. He is well rid of her and perhaps even regrets leasing that estate so near Longbourn since it led to this unrequited infatuation. But that's all I can say on that."

Darcy was again up, his glass left on a side table.

"Damn, Richard, had I only rejected my first instincts with that woman and the idiotic abhorrence I had about her family and her circumstances and allowed the truer, more honest feelings I had for her to grow, I know I could have convinced her to have me. And now I am all anxiousness about the thought of seeing her, of being in the same room with her after this time."

With that, Fitzwilliam Darcy turned on his heel and abandoned his cousin to fend for himself when the Colonel was called into the drawing room to make conversation with his aunt and the cousin, Anne, who seemed destined to soon become Mrs. Fitzwilliam Darcy, the mistress of Pemberley.

Chapter 4. Mrs. Collins's Regret

Not a mile from the events just recited, the object of the gentlemen's conversation was herself ill at ease. Her husband had given her the fine news that they were invited to Rosings itself for dinner the next day and that they were to be graced to be in the company of Lady Catherine's nephew Fitzwilliam Darcy, whom they'd both met in Meryton, and a separate nephew who was a Colonel who neither Collins had met.

Mrs. Collins was strangely affected by this news. She'd not thought, at least was not conscious of thinking, of Mr. Darcy much or deeply since those days long ago when they crossed paths when Darcy's great friend Charles Bingley leased Netherfield. Indeed, the whole lot of them vanished with barely a by-your-leave, and Elizabeth's older sister Jane confessed in her letters that she was prone to moments of melancholia from that disappearance and the subsequent intelligence that he had no intention of returning.

Now, with dinner over, Mr. Collins suggested he read something to his wife while she did needlepoint, as was a common way they spent their evenings. Elizabeth demurred, though, saying she wished to write to Jane. Her husband accepted this and sat in the front parlour with one of his books and was contentedly reading as Elizabeth extracted some stationery and pens from the desk that sat in the corner. She sat down to write to her sister, the light of a single candle being sufficient and appropriate for the intimacy she felt.

Dearest Jane,

I hope you are well. I confess to you that I do not know if I am.

I have just received the most startling news. Do not worry, it is of no significance except, perhaps, to my heart which I find is rumbling and trembling in a manner I have not known it to for so long.

Mr. Collins advised me with some excitement while we were at dinner that Lady Catherine has two visitors and that we are to be honoured to dine with them tomorrow at Rosings Park. I will not long tease you. The two are Fitzwilliam Darcy and his cousin, an unknown colonel who is related in some manner to both Darcy and Lady Catherine.

You'll recall that Darcy is Lady Catherine's nephew and, according to what Mr. Collins said upon delivering the news to me, he is destined to marry Lady Catherine's daughter. That is Anne de Bourgh, of whom I have made reference as a small, rather sickly creature of great financial worth and, so far as I can make out on the evenings when I have been with her at Rosings House or when she has deigned to stop while passing the Parsonage, little else.

But Mr. Darcy.

He was such a disagreeable man when I met him—as you and everyone else agreed—that I at least was pleased when he disappeared from Netherfield and Meryton soon after I committed myself to Mr. Collins. I am sorry to bring up what I know is a difficult period for you, but I fear I must explain the difficult period through which I am going.

You see, the mention of Mr. Darcy's name and the prospect of again seeing him has roused something in me that I did not know existed, or at least that I did not know existed since I have become a married woman.

Oh Jane. I must take care as Mr. Collins is not ten feet from me as I write this, quietly reading aloud some sermon or another. I cannot but tell you that the time apart from Mr. Darcy and the time during which I have not given a thought of him has allowed the fermentation of something truly womanly. I fear what might become of me the moment we are together, when we are introduced and I must feign complete indifference which is, I fear, the exact opposite of what I <u>will</u> feel.

I know this is insanity. I know nothing can come of it. I know so many things, but I cannot help but know my heart.

I write in the hope that this fever may break between now and when I curtsey to him, and he bows to me. I know he is completely indifferent to my existence. He never indicated by word or deed the slightest interest in me as other than a curiosity. Of being a country girl with something of an independent streak. Of some attractiveness but not nearly enough to tempt him.

I so wish you were here with me again. That we could walk along the paths around the Parsonage and talk in the manner we did as children, though the subject will be that of women.

My only hope, dear Jane, is that the reality of Mr. Darcy proves far less than my imaginary Mr. Darcy has become. Yes, I am sure that is the case. He was an unattractive man when I met him—save for his looks and his money!—and I am sure he still is. He was indifferent to me then as I am certain he is indifferent to me now. I should not be the least concerned that whatever ember once was present in my heart has long since been extinguished.

It is only that I fear that to the contrary it has been smouldering and smouldering and that it will burst into flames the moment it meets the oxygen of the presence of Fitzwilliam Darcy.

As what happens will have long since happened when you read this, I am not sending this letter to you. I do not know what I will be able to say in twenty-four hours' time. I do not know if I will be able to say <u>anything</u>. But I am afraid, Jane. I believed I was sufficiently content in the world fate had conspired to create for me. Now, though, I am afraid in a way that I have never before known.

Love,
Elizabeth

"Are you finished my dear?" Mr. Collins asked when he saw his wife blow on the page to help dry the ink. "I hope you sent my regards to your sister."

"Of course, my dear, I have done. As I always do."

Mr. Collins rose, and Elizabeth lifted the pages to shake them dry and he could not see her words.

"Very good, my dear," her husband said, as he came to her. "I am tired—perhaps from all the excitement about tomorrow—and am retiring. I wish you good night."

He gave his wife a kiss on the cheek before carrying his tract in one hand and a candle in the other to retire to his bedchamber.

When he was gone, Elizabeth Collins looked at the letter. It had served its purpose. There was a small fire in the grate. She placed the pages on top and watched as they crinkled away and then opened the window slightly to allow the smoke to vanish into the Hunsford night.

Chapter 5. Elizabeth's Walk Interrupted

I t rained heavily in the early hours of the next morning. When Mrs. Collins looked out into the lane from her bedchamber, the opening in the pales that led to Rosings was hardly visible in the fog. It was going to be a very uncomfortable day with the thick air, but she could not remain indoors.

Sitting down in the breakfast parlour with her husband, she saw how anxious he too was. No. It was more that she heard it. He continued speaking nearly without taking a breath about how excited he was ("my dear") for the upcoming trip to the great house and how excited he was ("my dear") to be seeing Mr. Darcy after having met him in Meryton and how excited he was ("my dear") to witness the two "lovers" enchant one another. This final image, of Darcy and Miss de Bourgh, only added to Elizabeth's unease about the evening's events.

By the time breakfast was done and the housemaid had cleared it away, the sun had burnt off most of the fog and was breaking through what was left of the clouds. Elizabeth suggested that she would like to go for a turn around the grounds.

"I think it might be rather warm, my dear," her husband observed. She thanked him for his concern but said she was quite determined, and she promised that she would not strain herself. As usual, then, he was content to sit in his small library with some of the sermons he was of a mind to reread until it was full day, when he would be able to venture into his garden.

She went out, lightly dressed and wearing a small bonnet, and onto the grounds where she expected she could walk undisturbed for upwards of an hour.

Her preference was to keep far from the great house so as not to interfere, though she knew that neither Lady Catherine nor Miss de Bourgh ever strayed far on foot. This left her tremendous privacy and solitude, which she often found lonely being without Jane or Charlotte Lucas (now Mrs. Sebel, a lawyer's wife) from Meryton.

On this solo walk, her mind was full, and her stomach was anxious about the trip to the de Bourghs' in under eight hours' time. The sun was getting high and the air warm. She would soon need to return to the Parsonage. As she rounded a corner into a brief shaded copse, she found herself approaching, or being approached by, a gentleman in a plainly agitated state, gesturing randomly and looking at the ground not five feet ahead of him and no farther.

The pair were within twenty feet of one another when he sensed that he was not alone. For her, so abrupt was his appearance that it was impossible to avoid his sight. Their eyes instantly met, and the cheeks of each were overspread with the deepest blush.

Each recognised the other at once. They exchanged the formalities of a bow (his) and a curtsey (hers). He spoke first.

"Miss Eliz...Mrs. Collins. I regret interrupting your solitude."

"So, you recall me then," Mrs. Collins responded, perhaps sounding more cynical than she intended. She attempted a smile. "Mr. Darcy."

He reddened further but was at a complete loss for words until without saying anything at all, he recollected himself, and with a bow took leave and was gone.

Mrs. Collins watched him disappear around the corner whence he'd come. *How did he recollect such slight passing encounters we'd had so long before?*, she thought. *Lady Catherine*, she calculated, *must have mentioned that her vicar and his wife were coming to dinner that night and likely he recalled that that wife was the former Miss Elizabeth Bennet.*

As she stood there watching where Mr. Darcy had vanished, all a muddle.

There was a small bench near to where she'd stopped, which she reached as she slowly began her walk back to the Parsonage. It was not truly a bench but had been the remains of a fallen tree that had been fashioned so it served as a seat. They were sprinkled about Rosings Park, and this one had a view out across a large expanse of lawn to the great house. And as she made herself as comfortable as she could make herself under the circumstances, she saw well on the other side of that lawn a rapidly moving figure heading with determination to the house.

Chapter 6. An Awkward Evening

"Oh, Mrs. Collins," the hostess (who remained seated) called as Mr. and Mrs. Collins entered the large drawing room of Rosings that evening, "You must be properly introduced to my nephews."

Stepping forward from the left side of her ladyship were two gentlemen. One, of course, was Mr. Fitzwilliam Darcy. The other, Mrs. Collins soon learned, was Colonel Richard Fitzwilliam.

"I have had the honour of meeting Mrs. Collins only last year, when she was still Elizabeth Bennet," Darcy said over his shoulder to his aunt, as he and the Colonel bowed, and Mr. and Mrs. Collins reciprocated.

"Darcy. You never told me that. But I suppose there's much you keep from your aunt."

"My dear aunt," Darcy returned, slowly releasing his eyes from the former Miss Elizabeth Bennet. "I do not 'keep' things from you, as you suggest. It is simply that I do not wish to trouble you with the trifles of my life."

"Oh, Darcy. Do not be so unsociable. You know that all your affairs, and those of your dear cousin, are utmost among my concerns and interests."

She turned to Elizabeth. "This is especially true, Mrs. Collins, as he is destined to marry my daughter."

"So I am led to understand," Elizabeth said as she and her husband shuffled to sit on a settee to Lady Catherine's right, beside Miss de Bourgh and Mrs. Jenkinson (a sort of minder for the daughter). Darcy and the Colonel mirrored this, settling to the Lady's left.

And the evening progressed well enough. Lady Catherine's attentions were acutely on her nephews. She expressed scant regard for anyone else in the room then or later when they all sat for dinner.

Lady Catherine had, early on, learned that Elizabeth played with some moderate skill on the pianoforte—an instrument on which she claimed she would have been proficient had she only had the opportunity to apply herself—though she'd never been able to discover her parson's wife to have any other particular or noteworthy talent. On this evening, she instructed Mrs. Collins to perform for the others.

And Elizabeth played some Italian songs and a Scottish air in an easy and unaffected manner in a corner away from the others and was largely ignored by them except for those moments when she happened to notice Darcy looking in her direction. When she struggled with the sheets of music, Lady Catherine instructed Mr. Collins, "Oh, go and help your wife turn the pages," but before that good man could place his dessert plate down, Darcy was up with an "I will do it." Four or five strides later, he was beside her, helping organise the papers.

"Thank you, sir," Elizabeth said, and he nodded and stayed standing slightly to the side to prepare for the next change and at the appropriate moment reaching across to do the page turn, his hand coming not unpleasantly near to her face as he withdrew it.

Elizabeth was, with more of a struggle than there should have been, able to concentrate on the notes before her and not the man beside her. When she finished a short Purcell transcription, he complimented her, *sotto voce*.

"You play very pleasantly."

As she placed the music for a Mozart sonata before her, and directing her voice at the music, she said, "You are far too kind, Mr. Darcy. There is much wanting in my technique."

"Yet," he said as she turned to him, seeing something of a pleasing smile, "were I forced to choose I should prefer the playing with a spirit such as yours. It is, I think, more enjoyable for that."

"You are being too kind, sir," she replied, "but I do thank you for your compliment and assistance."

She smiled as she began the piece.

"But I think you, sir, must return to your aunt's audience."

Elizabeth nodded to the group sitting on either side of Lady Catherine just as that good woman called, "Thank you, Mrs. Collins. Darcy. Come back to me."

Darcy bowed and turned towards the others and Elizabeth noticed his shoulders slumping as he reached them and resumed his seat near Miss Anne, by which point Lady Catherine was well into saying something to Colonel Fitzwilliam.

Elizabeth kept her eyes on Darcy. *Oh, how uncomfortable yet natural you look*, she thought as she herself rose presently to join her husband, who was hanging onto each and every word of her ladyship's pronouncements. And she found comfort in being safely ignored by virtually all the others for the balance of the evening.

Chapter 7. Darcy's Disappearance

Unlike the day before, the following morning broke clear and warm. Although Lady Catherine had a carriage carry them home, the Collinses were somewhat groggy as they sat for their breakfast. Their quiet, though, was interrupted by the sound of horses passing in the lane, heading from the great house to Hunsford. They were not going particularly fast but did not slow as they passed the Parsonage. Mr. Collins rose to watch.

"It is the two gentlemen, the two nephews," he called over his shoulder to his wife, who immediately rose to join him at the window, but only in time to see the rears of the riders and the animals disappear to the right.

"I wonder why they leave so early," she said. "They made no mention of them going so soon."

"Indeed, they did not, my dear, indeed, they did not."

The couple returned to their chairs to finish the meal, and as they did, Mr. Collins said, "it is truly a mystery and I suppose we must be patient to learn the reason if it is a sudden change in what was planned."

For her part, Elizabeth was completely at a loss.

"Perhaps they are simply running some errand in town and will shortly return."

"I am sure you are right, my dear. But I saw full saddle bags. Perhaps it is as you say and, in any case, there is nothing for you or me to do about it, even if their affairs were of any matter to us."

"Which they are not."

"Yes, my dear. Which they are not."

With that, the two prepared for another typical day for a Kentish clergyman and his young wife.

Chapter 8. Anne de Bourgh Writes a Letter

Several weeks after Darcy and Colonel Fitzwilliam departed so hastily from Rosings Park, the Colonel received a letter. It brought unfortunate tidings for the officer, which he promptly shared with his cousin.

"I must be off to America, my friend," he said.

"Surely the skirmishing there will soon be over, will it not?"

"Well, Darcy, I hope that it shall but nevertheless His Majesty has directed that I and the rest of my regiment sail in under thirty days. I daresay it won't last long once we somewhat hardened regulars arrive and at least we won't be going at Bonaparte. But arrive we must and, therefore, I must leave you and my hopes for a quiet and peaceful retirement. At least for now."

"Well," Darcy said, largely recovered from the shock of the news, "it is too far to Pemberley, and I think it best in any event that we return to Rosings Park."

"If you have been able to cure the hasty departure not long ago."

"I have apologised to our aunt and our cousin and explained that my return to town could not have been delayed for a moment."

"It is well that they never learned the true nature of your emergency."

"And I believe they never need to, as you well understand."

"Darcy, as always, I am at your disposal, but I agree that it will do us both well to return there before my compelled absence from England."

"It is the fate of an officer in His Majesty's Army."

"It is, indeed."

"I will write soon and advise Lady Catherine that we will, subject to her invitation, be arriving in three days' time."

"And what of cousin Anne?"

"I cannot now say. I do not think we have a choice but to travel to Kent."

And agreement having been reached, a letter was dispatched to Rosings Park and the two began preparing to accept Lady Catherine's certain invitation.

The invitation in fact came the day before they planned on departing. But it was not what they expected. It was from Anne, in a very precise hand with an elaborate seal. After reading it, Darcy passed it to the Colonel.

Rosings Park

My Dear Cousins,

We are pleased to have heard of your returning so soon after you were forced to abandon us, though we regret the circumstances that compel it. We are particularly excited about seeing our cousin before he departs for America.

We are, of course, pleased that you wish to return. My mother has, however, charged me with conveying to you both an item of loss that, I assure you, should not alter or hamper your visit but that, she believes, you should be made aware of so that certain trappings do not come as a surprise to you when you arrive.

It is that our clergyman, Mr. Collins, is dead. You met him on your prior visit. His death was accidental and a shock as well, involving a fall, tragically, at the House while he was running some sort of errand. It appears—so we have been told by the footman who found the poor man beyond recovery at the bottom of one of the House's staircases—that he was returning to the main floor after having collected (as he had leave to do) a volume from one of the rooms on an upper one while my mother and I were out and was startled by our unexpected return. He appears to have rushed to greet us and hurried more than he should have and tripped on a bump in the carpet at the very top of the flight.

A yard or a foot or so either side would not have sent him down but, alas for the poor man, his foot found the one spot that led to his horrible plunge. I am to understand that the unfortunate footman who discovered him was reacting to the poor parson's scream as it echoed up the stairs and about the foyer.

The House, of course, has entered a period of mourning, which will extend for the time that you are here. I suggest that you arrange for the sending of appropriate garments for your visit and accept that certain of the activities you likely expected to partake in will not be possible.

In any case, we will be quite happy to see both of you again and we will only regret the brevity of your visit. Since Mr. Collins is to be committed to his final resting place in the church's graveyard on Thursday, we think it best that you delay your arrival until Saturday next.

I can assure you both that my enthusiasm in this regard, however tempered by the sad news I am compelled to convey to you, is shared by my dear mother.

I remain your dear cousin, &c.
(Miss) Anne de Bourgh

When he was done, the Colonel handed it back to Darcy, who'd been watching carefully for this cousin's reaction.

"Well," Fitzwilliam said, "it is quite a sad story, though I will admit not to have taken much of a liking for the man. He seemed, I'm afraid, rather stupid and obsequious."

"Indeed," Darcy agreed. "But do you not think it an omen?"

The Colonel was surprised. "Darcy, you are virtually engaged to our cousin. It is what was always expected. Surely you cannot mean—?"

"I do not know what I mean. I only know that I do not have time to determine what I mean."

Darcy stood. He stepped to the window and looked out. His cousin stared at his back, leaving it to Darcy to say whatever it was he wanted to say. After some moments, with the only sound being from the horses and people on Brook Street, Darcy turned. "I am very glad you have come, Fitzwilliam. But I think I will need your help in determining what I mean."

"You? Asking for my help? My, that is a change. Darcy, though. You know I have no more experience with matters of the heart than you do. I know of dalliances. I know of...other types of meetings. But *love*? I shall only know it if it comes with fifty-thousand. I've not the luxury you have of falling in love where my heart decides it will fall in love. I am certainly not the one to have an opinion about the woman you suggest is the least bit relevant. The woman who was married to the parson."

"Elizabeth Collins."

"Yes, the one you had such regrets about. I do remember that, you see. I will tell you now as your friend and your cousin that your fate is and has long been tied to Anne and I think it a grave mistake for you to upset the apple cart for some imaginary attraction to some recent widow who is still suffering and will in any case be long in mourning.

"You," the officer continued as he watched his cousin pacing, "are getting no younger, my friend. You best put this 'omen,' as you call it, right from your head and instead confirm your commitment to marry Anne and be done with it. She will be more than adequate to become the mistress of Pemberley and though frail I daresay she will do well in the task of getting you an heir."

Darcy resumed his seat.

"You are right, of course. It was well, however, for me to hear it from someone I trust. Yes, I will express my condolences to the widow if she is still there and shall make my attentions as to Anne clear to Lady Catherine and that will be the end of it.

"Yes, I am very happy for your words of wisdom, my friend. Very happy."

Chapter 9. Darcy Goes to Rosings

The funeral for the late Rev. William Collins was a simple affair. He had no immediate family other than his wife and, in a sense, his parishioners. Mr. Bennet and Mr. Gardiner represented the Bennet family while the lady Bennets, all but Mary, who was too far away—she'd married a clergyman with a small living outside Winchester who see met at services when she was briefly visiting the Gardiners and he was visiting his own parents—stayed with Elizabeth at the Parsonage during the services. Sisters Kitty and Lydia had ridden up from Colonel Forster's house, in which they were guests, in Brighton. Jane traveled down with the Gardiners. That evening, all but the Gardiners and Mr. and Mrs. Bennet squeezed into the Parsonage, the others taking rooms at the fine inn in Hunsford.

A vicar from a neighboring parish performed the services in the church and in the churchyard. And then it was done. The earthly remains of the Right Reverend William Collins were safely in the ground and covered in dirt in the area reserved for those who had served as parsons for the parish, dating back well over a century and a half. While there was a spot for the vicar's widow when she reached the inevitable fate of all humans, Mrs. Collins doubted that she would ever be laid to rest there.

All of Elizabeth's family were gone the next morning excepting Jane. She would remain until it was time for the young widow herself to go. And they took a stroll that very afternoon. It was overcast as the pair entered the Park and with few words strolled with their arms interlaced until they'd completed a circle that brought them back to the Parsonage. And after some light refreshments, Elizabeth retired to her room briefly and rose again some hours later as the light began to fade while Jane slept in her small room nearby.

Chapter 10. Elizabeth Leaves Rosings

Early on the afternoon of Saturday, a carriage brought Darcy and Colonel Fitzwilliam to Rosings Park. Their passing by the Parsonage went unnoticed because both of the Bennets were again walking on a favoured path. This time on this walk, they spoke quite extensively but inconclusively about what Elizabeth intended to do. It would not be long before she would be compelled to leave the Parsonage and for a time at least settle back as a widow at Longbourn.

The sisters were near enough to the great house, though, that they saw the carriage's arrival but not so close that they could recognise who had come beyond that they were two gentlemen. It hardly mattered to them.

Early that afternoon, though, Elizabeth was interrupted as she toiled in her husband's garden. It was never hers and would soon be someone else's. Yet there was comfort there for her, in the solitude and in the working with her hands. The sun was high and the sky clear, so she wore a large, brimmed straw hat. Jane was in her room, napping.

"Mrs. Collins?," Elizabeth heard. She rose to face the visitor. He stood with the sun behind him so to her he was a silhouette, made even harder to see because strands of her hair had become dislodged and hung across her face alongside her nose. She attempted to clear them away with the back of her hand with only partial success.

He'd stopped at the slight stone wall that separated the yard from the lane.

"It is I, Mr. Darcy."

Elizabeth was surprised at the tall man's appearance and embarrassed about her own.

"Mr. Darcy? What...what are you doing here?"

"May I?" he asked with a slight bow as he stepped to the gate in the fence and he was through it as she said, "of course."

He, too, was surprised. She'd never been so attractive. He'd long viewed her as the type of woman who had some quite appealing features—in her case it was especially her dark eyes—but who in the whole was far superior in the combination of the elements. Somehow this was even more the case in the disheveled manner in which she now stood before him, her forearm attempting to shield the sun as she curtseyed. He gave another bow.

"I am here to express my condolences for your recent loss."

"Thank you, sir," she said. Catching herself, she quickly asked whether he would like some refreshments, especially given the warm air and the clear strain of his walk from the great house.

"Thank you, yes," he said, and she put the small spade she held on a table by the Parsonage's front door and went inside as he waited, slightly pacing back-and-forth on the path that led to the house itself.

After some time (at least to him) she returned, telling him that some water would be brought out.

A wooden bench sat against a low stone wall that defined the plot's small yard, the border opposite "Mr. Collins's" garden. Once the sun passed midday it enjoyed the shade of an old oak tree whose age no living person knew. On that afternoon, it was quite cooler than the open parts of the yard, and Mrs. Collins and Mr. Darcy each felt immediate relief from the press of the sun and the still air.

"I did not know your husband particularly well, of course, but I was quite distressed when my cousin, Anne, sent me word of what happened to him. I am very sorry for you and your loss."

"Thank you, sir," Elizabeth said. "It was so very sudden, and I am only now getting over the shock of it and trying to prepare myself for what will become of me."

"He had little money, I understand, if I may be so indelicate."

"Not at all. It is, I assure you, sir, foremost in my mind. He had the living but that will go to someone else. The reality is that there will be little for me. My poor parents do not know who will succeed to my husband's rights to our estate in Hertfordshire—"

"You mean Longbourn."

"Ah. I see you recall that as well."

"It was part of a quite pleasant period at Netherfield."

"Which was ended so abruptly."

One of the two remaining servants, little more than a girl, brought a tray on which sat a pitcher of water from the well in the rear and a pair of glasses. She placed it on a table on one side of the bench. She poured each a glass and curtseyed and left after handing them to the sitting pair.

"Our leaving Netherfield at that time was unavoidable, I'm afraid."

"Indeed. And I wondered, as did my sister Jane, who is resting upstairs as we speak, that you did not have the opportunity to return."

"Your sister Miss Bennet is here?" Mr. Darcy was genuinely surprised.

"She would not allow me to be alone."

"And is...is she married?"

"She has become very particular, has my sister. She, not unnaturally, believes she should have the opportunity to marry for love. Though with my changed circumstances that may no longer be possible."

The conversation had suddenly, for Darcy, veered into treacherous waters but he managed to alter its course.

"Have you learned who succeeds your husband as to...Longbourn?"

"Not as yet. Mr. Collins, my Mr. Collins, was an only child so I assume it must be some even more distant cousin of mine. But we do not know who he is or anything about him."

"Do you wish me to make inquiries?"

"I cannot see what your inquiries can tell us, sir, though I appreciate the offer. I suppose we must wait until he is located and contacts my father and, frankly, we are all very, very anxious about it. There is, though, nothing for us to do but, as I say, wait."

The two had refreshed themselves and were becoming comfortable when Darcy abruptly stood.

"I have taken up too much of your time, Mrs. Collins. I shall leave you and wish you well."

He bowed and she quickly joined him on her feet and curtseyed.

"Please give my warmest regards to your sister," he said and before Elizabeth could respond, Mr. Fitzwilliam Darcy was through the Parsonage's gate and crossing to the opening in the pale across to the path that would lead him back to the great house.

* * * *

WITH BUT A FEW DAYS remaining at her home, the widow was determined to enjoy them as well as she could. She still walked, often with Jane, but restricted herself to paths that went away from the great house and did not again see it, or its occupants or one particular of its guests.

Only two or three days later, a footman from the House appeared in the late morning. He did not have an invitation to dinner, but an envelope addressed in a delicate, precise script to:

Mrs. William Collins
Parsonage
Hunsford, Kent

She broke the elaborate, Rosings seal and unfolded the sheet.

August 16, 1812

My Dear Mrs. Collins,

My mother has employed me to write of the arrangements that she has instructed be made for your return to your own family. The Parsonage must be prepared for the new vicar and though we do not know who that will be or when he and his family will arrive, we must be prepared to act on it in an instant, as my mother is certain you understand.

By a fortunate twist, my mother intends to send a carriage to London in three days' time and is willing to have you ride in that conveyance to town, though you will be required to make arrangements for such other of your goods that cannot fit and that you wish to have sent on to wherever it is you intend to reside.

She assumes, of course, that all of the Parsonage's furnishings will remain <u>in situ</u> though as a gift she offers you *the opportunity to remove one piece to have as a remembrance of the house.*

My mother and I both regret immensely the need for you to leave us but as your dear, late husband would surely say if he were still among us, the Lord works in mysterious ways indeed.

My mother and I also hope that we will have the opportunity to visit with you briefly before your departure but if we cannot, I assure you that you have our best wishes with respect to what is to befall you in the future.

Yours, &c., &c.
(Miss) Anne de Bourgh

In fact, the schedules of Lady Catherine and her daughter were such that they could not manage a visit to the Parsonage, even a brief one. Nor did Mr. Darcy or Col. Fitzwilliam appear. And on the designated day, one of the lesser of the de Bourgh's carriages, in fact the barouche that first took Elizabeth to Hunsford, rolled to the front of the Parsonage. It was empty and when Elizabeth asked the coachman whether he would be going to London other than to carry her there, he said, "I know nothing about that, ma'am. Alls I know is whats I was told and that was to collect you and drop you at the stage in London to head up to wherever you be going, though none told me where that might be, ma'am."

The young widow did not have much other than her clothes, and these had been packed somewhat haphazardly into a pair of trunks, and there was room enough left for her to squeeze her books in as well as a small watercolour she eventually selected from the household furnishings as her sole (physical) memento of the place. There wasn't enough to require that a wagon or other conveyance be ordered—and paid for—so she was glad for the room and the two trunks were lashed to the rear of the carriage. With a single look back, Elizabeth Collins, as was Elizabeth Bennet, and her sister Jane, as still was Jane Bennet, were gone from Rosings Park and the Parsonage forever.

And from Mr. Darcy, too, who, for reasons he could not explain to himself or to Colonel Fitzwilliam as they headed back to town had not made an offer of any sort to his other cousin.

Chapter 11. Elizabeth Goes to Longbourn

Each sister was left to her own thoughts as they headed north in the old de Bourgh barouche as it rocked forward and side-to-side. Only as they approached London was there any significant conversation between them. Jane had delayed asking but could no longer refrain from doing so. *What in God's name would Elizabeth do now?*

It was a question uppermost in Mrs. Collins's mind but for all that it was no closer to receiving an answer now than it was when she first posed it to herself soon after learning of what had befallen her husband.

"You will be in mourning for some time, of course," Jane said after hearing nothing.

The pair were sitting opposite one another in the coach, Elizabeth facing the rear. Now she leaned forward and took her sister's hands in hers.

"Oh, Jane, I am so rattled by the possibilities for the future and then the understanding of how few they in the end are likely to be. My mind has been spinning without stopping on this. I wish only to fall into a quiet existence, however brief, in our parents' house till I must venture to wherever it is I will venture in the end."

"I did not intend to upset you, Lizzy," Jane said.

"Oh, forgive me. I know how you have been tried by the same thoughts and doubts about yourself for so long and now I throw myself at you as if I were the only one."

"But you are a new widow and that is so much different than I."

"I cannot admit to that. For I, too, have long been alone and perhaps it would be far different had I a child to love and who would love me—"

"Oh, Lizzy, I am certain that Mr. Collins did love you."

"Oh, I am sure of it, at least in his own way. He was a good man in the end. I sometimes think—and God forgive me for saying this—that he might have improved mightily had Lady Catherine vanished herself from his life. I do believe he might have improved himself but I'm sure he came to love me in his way. And that he might well have improved with a child. That did not happen. It was 'God's will,' he said, and I think he took comfort in that thought."

"I will leave it then," Jane said as the traffic was increasing, and the buildings grew more numerous and fancier and closer to one another. "Let us hope our father has sent the carriage in time so we shall not be long delayed."

In the event, the Bennet carriage had been ready to collect the girls for some thirty minutes when Lady Catherine's pulled into the agreed-upon meeting place just south of London Bridge. While the coachmen and footmen made quick work of transferring the baggage from one to the other, the Bennets took some tea in a tavern, sitting in its small yard off the road. Thus, in no time they were again on the road and as they approached Meryton their moods lightened, and Jane provided more gossip than Elizabeth could have any possible interest in. As they both knew.

Once settled at Longbourn, there was little that Elizabeth could do beyond receiving visitors from the village and from Meryton and once that was complete, she spent her days reading or sewing or practicing on the pianoforte in the house, though rarely attempting a piece that had the slightest chance of evoking happiness.

Jane remained with Elizabeth, and the two were often seen walking on the paths over which they had once trodden when they were a lifetime younger. And while ten miles was too far for even Elizabeth to walk, when the Bennet horses were not needed for working in the fields or some other task, at least once a fortnight she attached the lightest nag to a gig and visited dear Charlotte, just revealed to be in the family way when Elizabeth returned to Longbourn.

And Mrs. Bennet did in time recover once it was clear that Elizabeth did not carry the heir to Longbourn.

* * * *

A MONTH OR TWO AFTER Mr. Collins's death, Mr. Bennet received word from Lydia that he and Mrs. Bennet were to expect two very important visitors in only a few days' time. Lydia had gone to Brighton as the special guest of Colonel Forster's young wife when the militia had vacated Meryton for that seaside town. Kitty was allowed to follow some months later.

Having received Lydia's letter, Mr. Bennet asked Elizabeth to join him in his library and showed it to her.

"What thinketh thou of this, my dear?" he asked when she was finished and had lowered it.

"Oh, papa," she said as she handed it back. "They have surely gotten themselves engaged."

"What? Both of them?"

"It cannot surprise that if it's one it must also be two with Lydia and Kitty."

He sat in his preferred reading chair.

"I suppose you must be right. Perhaps in the end it was not a mistake, as I feared at the time it would be—"

"You never told me."

"Oh, Lizzy, you had enough with me seeking out your advice, however valuable you know I have always found it to be, every time one of your sisters wanted to do something. As I say, I may have been wrong in doubting the wisdom of permitting Kitty to join Lydia in Brighton, particularly after Lydia said she would surely find her sister a husband if she did. I think that must have been the case."

"Married to soldiers!," Lizzy laughed. "Mamma at least will be thrilled to see some redcoats in the family after losing that one she pined over so many years ago."

"Now, Lizzy, I don't need you reminding her of that period of life. I hear more than enough of it as it is."

"But there will be no escaping it. You know that."

He nodded, of course, for he well knew it.

"So now you must tell her about it," Elizabeth said in the tone reserved only for her father, "and I will tell Jane and we must prepare the house to be visited by two men who I assume are rich enough to marry paupers such as my sisters—"

"And which soldiers may have little sense if they wish to marry them."

"Oh, papa, you must not be prejudiced against them without at least having the opportunity to see them with your own eyes."

He stood and reached for his daughter's wrist, which he tapped before approaching the door with a "I will tell your mother now."

And at dinner Mrs. Bennet's excitement could not be suppressed even though the others insisted that it was only speculation that that was what was to be expected in the visitors the girls would be bringing.

"Oh, nonsense," she said. "They would not be coming all this way from Brighton with some flimsy excuse for a woman or two in tow. No, Mr. Bennet, they are surely going to be with the officers who will become part of our family. I promise you this."

There was no disagreeing with what was said, but at least Elizabeth was able to convince her mother that she, and the servants that they, should refrain from telling anyone outside the house, even her dear sister in Meryton, about it until the supposed and projected sons-in-law were at Longbourn and could be shown to truly exist.

"The credit will be much the greater, mamma," she said, "were the news to be delivered in the company of a pair of officers."

"Oh, I suppose you are right there. And they will be here soon enough. After waiting all these years for...for yet another of you to get married to a man of some distinction, I can wait a few days more, but only if they will be here before the end of the week. I cannot promise what I will or can say at church on Sunday so let us all hope they are all here by then."

And the fact was that they were all there by then. It was late in the morning, a quite cold Saturday morning it happened, when the rumble of the carriage reached Longbourn.

Mr. and Mrs. Bennet, both well bundled up, removed themselves from the house as the carriage came to a stop with a fine footman jumping down to open its door.

Lydia was the first out, Kitty right behind, and as if it were a race. Lydia rushed to her parents and said, "You never will guess who we have brought with us mamma, papa. It is a pair of very fine officers in very fine regimentals who have consented to take each of us as his wife."

"In any particular order, my dear?" Mr. Bennet asked.

"Oh, papa. The best one is for me, and his friend is for Kitty."

"I get the best one," Kitty said, but before anyone could react Lydia was calling to the carriage.

"Denny. Pratt. Come."

And like that a pair of, yes, what appeared to be very fine officers in very fine uniforms emerged. Mrs. Bennet recognised the two from when they were with the militia when it was staying in Meryton.

They stepped smartly to the Bennets and exchanged bows with Mr. Bennet before receiving Mrs. Bennet's slight curtsey. This was followed quickly by Mrs. Bennet referencing the cold and her old bones and insisting that sandwiches and meats and cheeses with ale had been set up in the front parlour with a warm fire for the valued visitors. Once the six were settled, Elizabeth came in awkwardly in her black dress. She recognised the two officers right away. They stood as she entered the room.

"Lieutenant Denny and Lieutenant Pratt. How good it is to see you again."

The two officers bowed quite deeply to who each expected would soon be a sister-in-law, and she exchanged a formal curtsey.

"Thank you, Mrs. Collins," Denny said. "May I express my...our condolences for the misfortune that has been visited upon you?"

"Thank you very much, Lieutenant. I appreciate it," and she gave a nod to Pratt as well. Elizabeth then turned to Kitty and Lydia and the three were joined by Jane and quickly greeted each other most informally until Elizabeth stepped back.

"I will see you all later but for now I am rather tired and must go to my room."

And she did see them later. At dinner, she heard all about their night in London at Denny's family's house in Bloomsbury and how Denny proposed to Lydia and the very next day Pratt proposed to Kitty. How Mr. Bennet sat with the two officers and was quite stern (and, for him, serious) with them about their responsibilities as husbands to his daughters. How Mrs. Bennet uncovered the general amount (and particular sufficiency) of their fortunes until someone observed the inappropriateness of such jovial conversation when in the presence of a woman only recently widowed. Things then became somber and less comfortable until all were relieved, particularly the widow, that Elizabeth excused herself to return to her room.

Neither Elizabeth nor her parents could go to the wedding ceremony itself in Brighton, but it was agreed that the ceremony not be delayed.

Jane and the Gardiners, then, represented the Bennet family and joined the others on a cold December morning waving at Lieutenant and Mrs. Peter Denny and Lieutenant and Mrs. Michael Pratt as they rode in their carriage for a week in Weymouth.

It had been an enjoyable event for all the participants, and with it over, Jane travelled back to London with her aunt and uncle and the next day continued on to Longbourn.

When Jane reached the house, her mother would not accept that her daughter was too tired from her travel to give details of the ceremony. Especially every detail of what her daughters wore and what winter flowers they were able to find to carry and place in their hair and how they wore that hair and who between the two was (confidentially, to be sure) the handsomer.

It was truly exhausting for Jane. Her mother finally accepted this and allowed Jane to return to her bedchamber so she could nap before dinner.

Chapter 12. Another Interesting Letter to Mr. Bennet

Early in the new year, on an unusually warm afternoon with the light fading and Jane back in London, Mr. Bennet again called Elizabeth into his library. When they were safely alone and she was in one of those favoured chairs of his, he opened a drawer in his desk and removed a letter.

"Lizzy," he said, "I will not delay in telling you this, but I have been contacted by the person who is to take this estate the moment I am dead. He seems a reasonable enough man, though I know nothing of him beyond what he decided to include in his letter."

He handed it to her.

"Please read it."

Lincoln's Inn
January 21, 1813

My Dear Mr. Bennet,

I have the honour of presenting myself to you. I am Archibald Collins and as you might surmise, I am closely related to the late William Collins. I am, in fact, his cousin, the son of his late father's younger brother. I have been advised by my solicitor that I have, as it were, stepped into my late cousin's shoes with respect to Longbourn.

I assure you that I write with the hope that you are well and will continue to be so for many, many years. I did believe it prudent, however, to make my existence known to you and your family as I expect there have been some anxious moments about who the new beneficiary of the entail on the estate might be.

I am myself a solicitor in London.

I understand that you had some less than pleasant dealings with my father's brother, by which I mean William Collins's father, and that my departed cousin endeavoured to atone for this as well as he could. I do not know whether you had any dealings with my own late father, but if you did, I hope that they were in fact on the pleasant side of the ledger.

In any case, I should like to visit you and your family at your convenience. As I am in London, it will take me little time to make myself available to you. I would only ask that you make some modest quarters available to me for a brief stay. I hope that once I have met you and your family, I will regret the brevity of my appearance and you will regret my hasty departure.

I look forward to your response.

I am, &c. &c.,
Archibald Collins, Esq.

As Elizabeth looked up, "Oh, preserve us, papa. Not another Mr. Collins!"

"Indeed, I expected as much but I knew nothing of him. I don't believe I ever did meet his father."

He reached towards her, and she handed the letter back.

"You did notice, I daresay, that he made no mention of any particulars on his account beyond his being a solicitor."

"I did indeed. Especially his failure to mention a wife."

"Well, I wonder if he too will come here in want of one, eh?"

"You cannot mean me!"

"Oh, Lizzy. You have done your duty. I can only hope that his affections go in another direction."

"Oh, papa, that leaves only Jane, and I am sure she will not bend to his will unless she truly has feelings for him."

"I know that, my dear. She has made that very clear while you were gone, that she'd experienced feelings she could not pretend she had not experienced."

"You mean as to Charles Bingley."

"Of course, though she will never let the name pass her lips and I do not dare mention him, though your mother sometimes does in very adamant terms, I must say."

"And of much pain to poor Jane."

"Well, Lizzy, we can hope that Mr. Archibald Collins is able to elicit some positive feelings from her, particularly now."

"Particularly now that I am again largely destitute and have become a burden."

Mr. Bennet rose and stepped to his favourite. "You will never be a burden on anyone, Mrs. Collins. Of that I can promise you."

She held her father's hand and raised it to her cheek.

"Still, one must eat, you know," she said.

He gently slid his hand away and resumed his seat.

"I know," Mr. Bennet said, "and I will always regret not being better at ensuring you would have something in the larder. But enough of that." He again stood, slapping his hands on his thighs. "We must hope and await the visit of Archibald Collins. I will advise your mother of his coming."

"And I must prepare for it as well," Elizabeth said as she stood.

After sharing the news with his wife, Mr. Bennet did as requested and wrote back to Archibald Collins and asked that if convenient he appear in a fortnight's time where he—Mr. Bennet—hoped that he—Mr. Collins—would enjoy visiting the estate and remaining for several days if he wished.

Elizabeth also wrote a letter to London, in her case to Jane, who was back on Gracechurch Street. She told chiefly of the news of the revelation of just who it was that would inherit Longbourn after their father was dead.

Jane was at Longbourn a week before Mr. Collins's expected arrival.

Chapter 13. Mr. Collins Comes to Longbourn

Archibald Collins could never have been mistaken for his cousin. He was not particularly tall (or short) or fat (or slim). He was in fact quite average in virtually all aspects. Yet he carried himself in such a manner as to make for a very pleasing overall appearance. He was seven-and-twenty years old with blondish/red pleasantly curly hair cut slightly longer than the normal.

When he stepped from his hired dark-green-with-gold-trim landau in the front gravel of Longbourn, his dress was fashionable but not *too* fashionable, good but not of the highest quality. He had not the slightest morsel of foppishness about him. He was a gentleman to be sure but plainly not a man of leisure, and a stranger would think him a lawyer or a banker or even a diplomat.

The four Bennets lined up, and Mr. Bennet stepped forward.

"Mr. Collins, I presume?"

"Indeed I am, sir, indeed I am. And I take it that this is the fine Mrs. Bennet," which caused her to blush at the attention, "and my cousins Miss Bennet and Mrs. Collins."

He reached for the latter's hand. "And may I express my deepest condolences, Mrs. Collins, for your loss."

"You are very kind, sir," she said as she felt a squeeze from the visitor's hand and perhaps, just perhaps, a dint of a smile at the sight of one or perhaps both of his cousins, or so Elizabeth thought.

"I did not know of my cousin's death, and you must excuse my failure to appear at his funeral."

"Again, sir, I completely understand."

Alas, Mr. Collins's visit could only extend for one evening as obligations in town required his prompt return. "The life of a young lawyer is a hectic one, Mrs. Bennet," he said when he advised his hostess of the unfortunate and unavoidable brevity of his being at Longbourn. "But as I have now met you and your delightful family"—he having been fully advised (several times by Mrs. Bennet) that the other three, younger daughters were well married—"I fear I may impose on your hospitality with some frequency going forward."

As Mr. Bennet found the heir quite a fine fellow, he was at least hoped he would come back. The extent to which the others shared this view is not known.

Given Mrs. Bennet's two objectives of, first, appeasing the person who could throw her out the moment her dear Mr. Bennet ceased to breathe and, second, finding suitable matches for her two remaining daughters (one still in mourning), she, too, desired his return.

Alas, those daughters were themselves uncertain about the man. He was, indeed, a fine gentleman, sufficiently fine that one wondered how it could be true that he was a cousin of the first of the Mr. Collinses who visited Longbourn.

Still, Jane recognised her own situation and as Lizzy had done earlier, understood that it could well fall to her to marry a Mr. Collins. She did quite like him, on first impression. He was young, passably handsome in his way, well off on a fine professional career with (he noted as if in passing) fine lodgings in an attractive part of London.

"I do take most of my meals at my club, you understand, but that would change should I have the good fortune of finding someone I could share my life with. And I do have a housekeeper who comes in three times in a week to keep things adequate for visitors."

When Jane came into her sister's bedchamber late on the day of Mr. Collins's departure, Elizabeth reflected on her own first impressions and said about their guest, "I think he came much as my dear husband did. I can tell you, Jane, that I cannot see myself developing any feelings for him."

"I once found myself too easily willing to have feelings for a man, but in time I could imagine having some for him. I truly do," Jane said.

"Then I hope that is true, Jane."

And with a smile, Jane left for her own room.

* * * *

WITH ARCHIBALD COLLINS gone after flitting across Longbourn, Jane insisted that it was time for Elizabeth to join her in London at the Gardiners.

"You've reached half-mourning, and need to begin the process of taking the first steps in returning to society."

"'Returning to society'? Oh, Jane," Mrs. Collins laughed. "I was never 'in' society, as you well know."

"Well then it is time that you make an effort to finally enter it. You are still quite young though a widow. I cannot see anyone of any sense looking down at you should you remarry in due course. I have spoken to our aunt, and she and I agree that if you are in London your chances of finding someone for whom you have feelings, enough to consider marrying—"

"Provided he has money enough as well."

"Indeed, you are no fool—"

"Though perhaps I was in marrying the first man who offered his hand to me."

"Lizzy, you cannot go on about that. We all know why you did, and we are all grateful for that sacrifice. I, at least, understand how difficult it must have been for you."

"Oh if you only knew. After some time, though, it became tolerable, if barely so."

She smiled as she grabbed and gripped her sister's hand. "But what's done is done and you are quite right. I think I must look to the future as neither of us is getting any younger, you know. Though I will insist that you will defy the laws of aging and could turn out even more attractive before you are thirty than you are now, if that is possible."

"You are too evil, Lizzy." But both reddened and both knew that Elizabeth might well be right.

Without having any particular scheme in mind, it was agreed that Jane was surely right in at least one respect. Elizabeth would go to town now that she could socialise if still only slightly. It was agreed by all, too, that there were no legitimate prospects to be found within ten miles of Longbourn, if not twenty.

Chapter 14. To Cheapside

Spring performed its annual ritual of coquettishly teasing London from the winter. While it was fine when Jane and Elizabeth reached Gracechurch Street, it was miserable for the several days thereafter. This delayed Elizabeth's ability to explore the neighbourhood such that by the time the weather cleared enough to allow her to wander, she was beyond enthusiastic.

On her first Tuesday, she declined Jane's offer to accompany her, with an assurance that she would surely be able to find her way back to the Gardiners'. And it was delightful, her walk interrupted by some quiet moments in a pew to the side and halfway up the nave of St. Paul's and by obtaining refreshment in the form of a light cake and coffee at a small shop on a side street that led to the church.

She tired more quickly than expected. Fortified by the cake and coffee, she was back on Gracechurch Street less than two hours after she'd gone out.

When Elizabeth stood in the foyer, and a manservant had relieved her of her coat and bonnet, Jane hurried to her.

"I saw you come up the street," she said. She waved a small letter in her right hand as she reached her sister.

"It is from our cousin, Mr. Archibald Collins." She handed the note to Elizabeth. "He inquires," said Jane, "whether the pair of us have any interest in joining him and a group of his friends for a dinner to be held at his residence on Thursday next at six o'clock."

Elizabeth looked up. "I see he is particular about me coming with you."

"Yes, he assures us that it will be appropriately somber given your situation. You must go with me," Jane insisted when she saw her sister's expression. "It is perfectly appropriate, and it is not so soon for you, particularly as it is being put on by Mr. Collins, who is our cousin."

"But what am I to wear?"

"This is true, of course. London is far different from Meryton, to put it mildly. But my aunt can go with us to a proper shop where we can find something fitting and appropriate."

Elizabeth retained her doubts, but Mrs. Gardiner proved quite adept at such tasks. Though it was far from the salons in the more fashionable parts of town, a fine dressmaker was enlisted, and a fine half-mourning dress that fell quite well over the young widow was obtained.

In the event, it more than sufficed. Mr. Collins and his guests, a mix of men chiefly from Lincoln's Inn and their wives, were very gracious to the sisters. For her part, Elizabeth kept herself observant and noticed the attention afforded Jane by Mr. Collins and several of the other gentlemen as well as the pleasantness of the conversation that the women had before being rejoined by the others.

The visit made, Mr. Collins returned it to the Gardiners', though being employed meant he came by out of hours that governed members of the leisure class.

Chapter 15. Mr. Darcy Meets Mr. Collins

It was a clear spring morning and as usual Darcy and Bingley were exercising their mounts on the outer ring of Hyde Park. It had to be cut short, Darcy warned his friend, because some legal matter concerning Pemberley required his personal attention. "Just some papers to sign," he said, "but what must be done must be done."

It was not much past midday when Darcy returned to Brook Street while Bingley continued to his house some streets to the south and west.

Suitably cleaned and refreshed, with some meats and cheeses with ale for a meal, Darcy was in his study when his butler, Bradley, knocked to advise that, "The lawyers are here, sir."

At his master's instructions, the two fellows were led in, the younger of the two carrying, over his arm, a bag laden down with documents.

After a standing exchange of bows and a declined offer of wine, with Reginald Chalmers introducing his junior, the two lawyers sat on one side of the large desk that was centered against one wall of the study, facing a broad window that opened out to Brook Street. Their client sat on the opposite side, his back to the window.

The older of the two, a tallish man of perhaps fifty who wore a wig, said, "Mr. Darcy, as you know there is a matter in Derbyshire that required that some action be taken against an individual who sought to squat at Pemberley. That dispute—"

"As I understood it, Chalmers, there was no 'dispute' about it at all. He set up some sort of camp on my estate and he was compelled, ultimately, to leave my land."

"Exactly right, sir. I appreciate your fine clarification. We had him ejected. To close the matter, the magistrate in Sheffield has instructed us to obtain your signature on some documents."

"It seems a rather foolish waste of time and my money on such a petty detail, do you not think, Chalmers?"

"I do think, sir, I do. But the law is a rather fearsome mistress, and she must have what she must have."

"I am all too familiar with that. Let us waste no more of our time than required. Just show me what needs to be signed and we can all be done with it and move on to more productive things."

"Of which there are an infinite number," the younger lawyer said, as he reached into the bag to remove the documents needing signatures.

To Darcy, this seemed an impertinent interruption. "I do not believe I know you, sir," Darcy said to the impudent attorney.

"I'm sorry Mr. Darcy, sir," Chalmers said, glaring at his junior. "Mr. Collins is a bit rambunctious, sir. You see—" (and while his lead was speaking, Collins was organizing the papers to facilitate their execution) "he's expecting soon to become engaged to what he says is a quite attractive young lady."

"Indeed, Mr. Collins. You have my sincere congratulations, though I've...I've yet to enter into such a pleasant situation."

"Oh, he's been a man of the world, Mr. Darcy." This was a bit of meandering conversation from Chalmers as he waited for his young colleague to put the paperwork in order. "He's decided the life he's been leading might be the early death of him."

"You are settling down, then?" Darcy asked.

"I figure" (this was Mr. Collins) "that it's time to at least get me some heirs before returning to my old ways."

"He just came into an inheritance, you see, Mr. Darcy," said Chalmers. "His cousin was to get an estate down in Hertfordshire when the current owner of the entail dies, he having no boys and, can you believe it?, five daughters."

"Yes, and they are married but the two oldest," said Collins. "The eldest is not married and the next in line happens to be the widow of my cousin, who died in a strange accident at the house of the lady who gave him his living."

"He was a clergyman, then?"

"Indeed, sir. I hadn't seen him for many years, our own fathers having something of a falling out, you see, and I'm told he was a bit of a pompous ass. But his very young widow seems nice enough."

"You've met her."

"Indeed. She and the other sister, who is an angel. She looks healthy enough to give me what I want and to allow me to enjoy myself doing it, if you know what I mean."

Darcy remained silent.

"So, you are interested in the older?" the client finally asked, just as Collins had arranged the papers as they needed to be arranged.

"Aye. The other one, my cousin's widow, is pretty in her way, I suppose, but I think she'd be less a wife than a tyrant, if you know what I mean. The other one's much more pliable and prettier. She's the one I've decided on."

"Has she decided on you?"

"Not as yet. But seeing as her family's going to be desperate when the father dies and the entail comes to me—which is why the sister married my cousin in the first place, you understand— I can't say she has much of an alternative."

"And the other sisters?"

"They've done well enough, Mr. Darcy—if you can just sign here—with the youngest two recently married to well-off officers in the militia and the other married to some clergyman with a nice living north of Winchester—and here—so I figure she'll have what we lawyers call a 'Hobson's choice,' which means no choice at all."

"I know what a Hobson's choice is, Mr. Collins," said Darcy as he placed his autograph on the final spot pointed to by the young solicitor.

"Understood, Mr. Darcy."

Chalmers interrupted.

"As far as the documents are concerned, you've signed them all, so I don't think we need take more of your time. Correct, Mr. Collins?"

"Indeed, we are finished, Mr. Darcy. I apologise for going on as I did. As Mr. Chalmers says, I am quite excited about this sudden change in my fortunes, in both money and, in its way, love."

He blotted the signatures before reassembling the documents as Darcy rose and stepped to the window and looked out, resuming his silence, ending it only when Chalmers called to him.

"Now, Mr. Darcy, I believe that is it for now. I do apologise for the interruption but—"

"But the law can be a fearsome mistress. Yes, Mr. Chalmers, Mr. Collins, I understand. Thank you for coming and being so comprehensive and, Mr. Collins, so informative."

He pulled the cord, and Bradley was in the library immediately.

"Bradley will show you out. Good day, gentlemen."

Though Mr. Chalmers attempted to further apologise for his junior's impertinence, Darcy waved him off, not wishing to extend the interview a moment longer than necessary.

"Again, thank you, gentlemen."

The two lawyers echoed, "Good day, Mr. Darcy," and then they were out and Bradley closed the door and Darcy stared out to Brook Street, pondering the information he'd just received and wondering whether it might prove of interest to his best friend, knowing he could not delay an hour or half of one to discover that.

When Darcy saw the two lawyers leave the house, he formulated his plan. First, though, he tried to remember where in Cheapside the Bennets' uncle lived, though thankfully the name had stayed with him. Without knowing at least that, he would have been lost with no plan at all.

He grabbed at an atlas of the streets of London. He knew little about Cheapside and if he had been there five times in his life he would have been surprised. As he ran his finger along the map of the area, getting more and more anxious at not finding the street whose name he'd only heard a few times from Bingley's sisters, it was there.

GRACECHURCH STREET

Yes, that was it. Within a minute, he was through the foyer telling Bradley he had an errand to run—"an errand to run, sir, that we cannot do for you?"—and within two he was on the pavement hailing a hackney cab, and within three he was hurrying onboard east into denser and denser London traffic.

As soon as they'd arrived at the wanted street, the matter turned to locating the desired house. This was far, far different from those parts of London with which Darcy was familiar. Men and boys, and the very occasional woman, racing hither and thither paying the fine gentleman no mind beyond navigating around him when he stood dumbly and in their way as they were going wherever it was that they were going.

He moved from the flow of the human traffic and came upon a haberdasher's shop. He went in and was set upon by a younger man who turned obsequious before the gentleman's eyes and begged to know what possible service could be performed in the 'umble shop.

"Thank you, man, but I merely am seeking to discover the address of someone I believe lives on this street."

With a nod, the shopkeeper's assistant said, "Very good, sir. And 'ho might that be?"

"The gentleman's name is Gardiner, I believe. He is a successful trader, though I've not met him."

"Gardiner you say?"

"Or something like that, yes."

"I don't believe I know that name, sir, but if he's done well for 'imself, he'd likely be living a bit aways from this part of the street. I suggest you go four or five blocks to the north and if he be there, they'll sure know where it is exactly."

With his own slight bow, Darcy thanked the shopkeeper for the help.

"Just turn to the right when you leave us, sir, and four or five blocks will get you close, I imagine."

With a final nod, Darcy was again on the pavement and joining the current of those people hurrying north on Gracechurch Street and avoiding those hurrying south.

After he'd travelled the suggested number of blocks, Darcy came upon a fine milliner's shop and when he, breathing heavily, entered, a clerk stepped up to him with a bow and asked how he could be of service. Three or four women were browsing and holding up and trying on hats and each of them turned at the appearance of the young and very fine gentleman before turning back their eyes (if not their ears) to what they were doing before the interruption.

"Thank you, good afternoon. I am looking for the residence of a Mr. Gardiner."

"'Gardiner' you say, sir? There be one only a block or two from here."

"I believe they have at least one niece living with them."

"I know them. Right now, there be a pretty unmarried one, who is often with them. And a second one, a poor young widow just come a few weeks ago. Still in half-mourning, she is."

"That would surely be them. Can you oblige me with the address, if you please?"

The customers were no longer bothering to hide their interest in this gentleman and what he was in their shop for and who it was he was searching for, though Darcy did not notice and had he noticed would not have cared.

"It is on this side of the street, sir," said his informant, "about two blocks. I can't remember the number—"

"It's seventy-two," offered one of the older ladies, standing with who was surely a reddening daughter, and the clerk said that that was surely it.

"Two blocks to the right, sir," he confirmed. On this side of the street. A blue door I think."

"It's red and not far from the Gardiner warehouse," corrected the woman, for which Darcy expressed his eternal thanks before bowing generally from the store and beating his retreat.

The lady informant called to him. "But I seen the two ladies, though not the wida, leaving as I was coming here so they ain't gonna be there if that's who you be lookin' to see."

Darcy gave another bow. "Thank you, ma'am. I believe I shall be fine."

Now I have the place and have luck working for me, Darcy thought as he resumed his journey. He was not certain, though, of what he would do when he reached it. He crossed Gracechurch Street, the better to remain unobserved.

There it was. Indeed, The red door evoking thoughts of a welcoming country church, though the house was clad in red brick and not stone. He stood for a minute, hoping to be inconspicuous among the passing pedestrians, their numbers reduced since he was a bit away from the more business-oriented blocks. With a deep breath, he checked the traffic and wove his way across. The bell was answered very quickly.

"I am here to see Miss...Mrs. William Collins on a matter of some urgency," he told Jones, the butler. He reached into a pocket and removed a card.

"Is she at home? I understand that her aunt and sister have gone out."

"They have, sir. I will inquire as to Mrs. Collins." The butler looked at the card and then back up, "Mr. Darcy."

"And her sister, Miss Bennet, is not here?"

"As I said, she is not. You know the family then, sir?"

"I do. It is a matter of some urgency as to Mrs. Collins."

"If she is available, I will advise her." The butler opened the doors to the sitting room when the quiet was interrupted by the sound of boys shouting from an upper floor.

The butler smiled at the interruption. When Darcy was established in the room that faced the street, the butler closed the doors and was gone.

His absence was brief though it seemed far longer to Fitzwilliam Darcy. He stopped his pacing when the door opened.

"Mr. Darcy, sir. I am all astonishment."

They exchanged courtesies.

"Am I to understand it concerns my sister Jane?"

"How did you—?"

"From your queries to Jones."

"Of course," he smiled. He was quickly reminded of how clever she was and how lovely those eyes of hers were. It took him a moment to recover. Yet recover he did.

"Mrs. Collins, it does concern your sister and I came here as quickly as I did because, frankly, I believe it may be of the greatest concern imaginable."

This quite disconcerted Elizabeth.

"Will you sit? May I get you refreshments? You look agitated."

"That is largely from my walking to get here."

"Will some air do you good? I'm sure it would me," she said.

He was glad for the suggestion. "The open air would do us good. I agree with you, Mrs. Collins. I also must assure you that I bring nothing concerning your sister's health or well-being except, if I might say, concerning the condition of her heart."

He had never spoken so, Elizabeth knew. *And about Jane?*

"It happens, sir, that I am prepared to go with you as I am."

And five minutes later, the two were beside each other and turning at the widow's suggestion onto a less crowded side street that would lead them to a small green that Elizabeth often circumnavigated in the morning before Jane was up.

When they reached the park, their conversation began in earnest.

"I came in some urgency in the hopes of speaking to you because I met with a Mr. Collins this afternoon on a matter of business."

"Collins? Archibald Collins? A lawyer?"

"Thank you for confirming it. He told me enough of himself to convince me that he has replaced your late husband—again, you have my condolences—as the presumptive heir to your family's estate."

"Indeed he is. We only met him some weeks ago when he wrote to my father and visited us for a day before he had to come back to town."

"I met him as a matter of business. He is a junior lawyer in the office of my solicitor and came when I had to sign some documents concerning my estate. He seemed a pleasant enough man, this Archibald Collins, but it struck me that he had not as many gentlemanly bones in his body as I would like in a man."

"So, you did not like him, then?"

"No, I did not. It was the very loose things he had to say. About himself and I'm afraid about your sister."

"Mr. Darcy. You can be a quite quick study of a man, I think," she said, while thinking *of a woman too, I know*. "But how does that concern my sister?"

"He made it very clear that he intends in the near future to make her an offer."

"I am not surprised, Mr. Darcy. She is quite a woman to be wooed and perhaps won, and you understand my family's financial predicament."

"I became further aware of it as he went on-and-on about you and your sisters. It was an additional unsettling thing about the man."

"That may well be, Mr. Darcy. But what interest can you have in the affairs of my simple country family?"

"Please don't patronise me, Mrs. Collins. I will get to the point."

The two stopped. They turned to face one another. And she for a moment wished there could ever be the prospect of him even being a friend to her in her very lonely world.

"Does your sister have feelings for Charles Bingley?"

Elizabeth's dark eyes grew. "Again, sir, what business is it of yours?"

"I will be direct. I believe that my friend has long regretted leaving Netherfield. Not because of the land or the countryside or the hunting. But because of your sister. He makes little effort to enjoy female company beyond in the most superficial ways. I have tried. His sisters have tried. All in vain."

"Does he speak of her?"

"Never. I cannot say he has spoken aloud the name of Miss Jane Bennet above five times since we came back to town. But I know he has thought of her."

"Does he know she is still not married?"

"I do not think he does since, again, I do not dare mention her name. Perhaps his sister Caroline provided him with that information, though how she would know or particularly care, I cannot fathom. They are in such different spheres. But to my question. Does she have feelings for him?"

They resumed the walk and were strangely but unconsciously closer to one another as they did.

"She is much as you suggest he is, from what I am given to understand since I was away for some time in Hunsford. But I know my mother has made every effort to find her a husband and my aunt as well, which is why she is so much in town. My aunt has told me how Jane is much as you describe your friend Bingley."

"And what of Mr. Collins?"

"This new Mr. Collins I believe may have a chance with her. He is in much the same position as his cousin was when I married him. It was the position of having to consider more than the heart."

"I am genuinely sorry for your sacrifice on that account."

"It could not be avoided, of course. It was a sacrifice in ways, but it was tolerable, and I was willing to tolerate it. Being a clergyman's wife in the living of a great woman who is rare in extending her attentions except on Sundays is not entirely unpleasant, you know. In addition to having the residual interest regarding my own parents' home."

"Do not fear me taking your reference to my aunt in those terms as being your honest view of her. She is my aunt and I love and respect her for that, but I am not blind to her deficiencies."

"Or those of her daughter, I daresay."

"Indeed. Of my cousin Anne. But this is not about anyone but my friend and your sister."

"Then I will be clear with you. I believe that she still in some ways has intense feelings for Charles Bingley. This is quite a surprise to learn that he may still have them for her after he left Netherfield and did not return and did not even visit her when she was in town. To the key object of this conversation, she has made no obligation to Mr. Collins, but I fear she will if she is asked to. I think that you and I, sir, must ally ourselves, however briefly, to prevent that obligation from arising unless and until we can establish that a different and more pleasant one cannot develop."

"I believe we are of one mind in this. Can you speak to your sister to at least defer any response to a question that may be made to her by her cousin without making a commitment with respect to Bingley that I cannot assure her will be made?"

"I think for at least a short time should Mr. Collins extend the type of offer you believe he will extend that I can convince Jane to beg for additional time to consider it."

Satisfied, Darcy said, "I will not keep you or her long in suspense. I will speak plainly to Bingley about it as soon as I can and if we both learn that our suspicions are correct, we can consider what possibilities there are to make them happy."

The pair separated after walking quietly from the green, when they were about a block from Gracechurch Street.

"Mr. Darcy, sir. I am forever in your debt for alerting me to this state of affairs."

"Mrs. Collins, allow me to add that from what this lawyer said, I would question his level of...commitment, not only to your sister, who is I think so innocent—"

"Unlike me, you say?"

"I have the greatest respect for both you and your sister, but I will not pretend that you do not have some broader experience of the world, having been married. And I fear Mr. Collins—*this* Mr. Collins—might not be the most faithful of spouses, though I perhaps may be wrong. I mean that as to your sister and as to any woman. I will say no more and hope I never have to.

"For now, I will be glad if I can have been of small assistance to your sister in this regard as well as to my friend. I shall probe him before you do the same with your sister. Someday, I may have the opportunity to speak to you further about them. For now, I leave you with my highest regard for you, your sister, and your aunt and uncle."

"Will you not visit us? You have not met the Gardiners I do not believe."

"I have not had that pleasure, to be sure. I think, though, that we best try to resolve what we can between Bingley and your sister before we do anything more."

"And how shall that be done?"

"As I said, I will speak to Bingley presently. To advise you of the results of that conversation, I will arrange to have a letter delivered to you personally at the Gardiners'. It will appear to come from a lawyer and advise you that there is some formality related to your husband's estate that requires your immediate attention."

"What sort of formality?"

"There is always something in these matters that needs signing, so it will not appear at all suspicious. You must endeavour to come alone to the address indicated. It will be to an office, by not to my solicitor's—"

"Because Mr. Collins is a lawyer there."

"Precisely. It will be from a different lawyer. If your sister must accompany you, so be it, though I prefer that she not. If she does, you will be advised to tell her that it is of a confidential nature, and you must be left to do it alone. I will then be able to provide you with such news as I have without, I hope, anyone else being aware of our connection."

"I understand."

"I am sorry that it is being done in this way, but I see no alternative. We cannot allow the principals to be aware until we are both assured that they are of similar views towards each other. I will first test Bingley's before you do the same with your sister."

"From what you say, sir, I do not doubt it."

"Nor, Mrs. Collins, do I. But we must be sure."

He gave a quick bow and turned and even before Elizabeth had taken a further step, he had disappeared into the pedestrians moving along the Gracechurch Street pavement.

Chapter 16. Back at the Gardiners'

Elizabeth was relieved when she returned to the house and discovered that there had been no visitors. Jane was home, though, and Elizabeth found her sister lying back on the white cotton counterpane that covered their bed, still in the dress she'd worn for her excursion. One of her boots was near the door and the other was against the chest of drawers on which her bonnet and gloves sat.

Jane bent herself up on her elbows to look at her sister. "Lizzy, where have you been? My aunt and I were quite unnerved when we saw you were not here. Jones said only that you had gone for a stroll somewhere."

Elizabeth removed her hat and gloves and placed them next to Jane's atop the chest, thankful for the butler's discretion. She dropped down onto the side of the bed, near her sister.

"I...I just required some air."

Jane plopped back down.

"Is that all? I thought you might have run off on us."

"Where could I possibly want to be when I can be here with you?"

"Pemberley, perhaps," she teased.

It was well that Jane did not notice her sister's fine eyes expanding for the second time in the last hour.

"Why...why would you say that?"

"Lizzy. Are you...flustered?"

"No. No, it's just that you say that. I've not thought of that place—which I note I have never come close to actually seeing, let alone walking the grand halls of—in a very long while."

Jane again positioned herself so she could look at Elizabeth.

"I meant nothing by it. It's just that while we were out, Aunt Gardiner mentioned having spent time in Lambton and that the town was a mere five miles from Pemberley. I don't think she knew that I'd ever heard of it or that it would raise such...complicated feelings in me so I let her describe it as we went from shop to shop until she thought my silence was my boredom and changed the subject."

"Well, I promise you," said Elizabeth after recovering from the surprising reference to Darcy's country estate, "and as you can see, I have assuredly not run off to that place you mention nor, I daresay, am I ever likely to."

Jane was satisfied with this response and let herself drop back on the bed.

"I wonder if Mr. Collins will visit tonight. Aunt Gardiner wonders that too."

"Have you reason to expect him?" Elizabeth said after she was yet again back on the small bench at the vanity against the wall.

"It's that I think he may be anxious to continue our acquaintance now that we are all in town."

"Well, I am sure he will visit us again with some frequency as I believe he is surely obligated to. But I expect it will be no more than a matter of courtesy and respect."

"Do you really think that?" Jane asked the ceiling.

"Why?"

Jane tired of lying on the bed and rolled so she could stand and then sat on it facing Elizabeth.

"I was quite taken by him. I really was. There was nothing that displeased me about his person or his manner and of course his relationship with my family."

Oh, were this a day before and how happy I'd be, thought Elizabeth. *Do I dare destroy this enthusiasm by mentioning another? The other?* She stood and paced to the window, looking down at the back garden. The greatest care was required.

"It is early days, Jane, but can we agree that you not act too precipitously?"

"Whatever do you mean?"

"Believe me. I felt the pressure from everyone concerning my Mr. Collins and I don't know what I would have done had I delayed the decision."

"You would have done exactly what you did. You had no choice. Any prospects I had with...Any prospects that *I* had turned out to be nothing in the end, passing dust in the wind, so it was well that you did marry."

"I do not want to return to that period. I am merely saying that I think it would be prudent for you to better understand this Mr. Collins before you make a decision that you cannot revoke."

"Assuming he will ask."

"Do not pretend that there have not been many who would have asked if you gave them the slightest encouragement, which you have consistently refused to do, as Aunt Gardiner has advised me on several occasions."

"Perhaps I have tired of being so stubborn, particularly given your changed circumstances."

They found themselves sitting beside one another on the bed.

"But I promise you this. I will not commit to anything with him or anyone else until you and I have consulted about it. Would that be agreeable to you?"

Elizabeth reached to put her arms around her sister. "Oh, that would be most agreeable indeed."

And with that the two got out of their walking clothes and, with the help of Bridget, the housemaid assigned to them, prepared for dinner.

* * * *

AS IT HAPPENED, THAT afternoon's little conversation between the sisters had the most desired effect for Elizabeth: Jane had agreed she would deflect any entreaties that Mr. Archibald Collins might make to her. That lawyer had stopped by the house after his work was completed for the day, though it was after dinner had concluded but, as he said, "needs must," and was welcomed to sit with the Gardiners and the Bennets.

He got on well with Mr. Gardiner and the two shared glasses of port together until they were joined by Mrs. Gardiner, Mrs. Collins, and Miss Bennet.

And the evening flowed delightfully for all concerned. Excepting Elizabeth. Her concentration was devoted to watching Mr. Collins closely and especially his interactions with Jane. But both were quite appropriate even as they displayed some certain flirtation towards each other. She was certain, however, that it would not be long before more intimate connections would appear.

That night, while Jane slept quite well and heavily, Elizabeth, beside her, did not. The bedchamber, at the back of the house, was very dark and all Elizabeth could do was sense the presence and calmness of the woman beside her. Her breath slow and regular and now it was Elizabeth who stared at the ceiling with which Jane had conversed those hours earlier. At some point, though, the exhaustion caught up with her and it was full day when Jane playfully pushed her sister to rouse her.

"I am going down for breakfast and you best get your bones up so you can have some before it is all gone forever," she said with a final push, and before Elizabeth could get back at her Jane was gone.

She didn't know what time it was, but the sun was well into the day's clear sky, and she hastened with Bridget to get downstairs and into the dining parlour. There her sister and aunt and the two oldest children, the girls, were eating and speaking.

After some teasing from Jane as to the lateness of her arrival and questions from her aunt about her plans for the day, Elizabeth began to relax and enjoy the company. With the children upstairs for their lessons and the breakfast done, Elizabeth and Jane went to the sitting room. It had a small bookcase, and the two tended to leave their books there since it had good light and comfortable chairs, much like Elizabeth's little room at the Parsonage. Jane, though, was much less a reader than was Elizabeth, who once confessed that she, too, was not herself a great reader during an evening at Netherfield.

After being in the room for perhaps an hour, Elizabeth saw a messenger approach the house. She froze, listening for what from the foyer could be heard through the door. After seeing the messenger leave, she said to Jane, "I must see to something," and with that she was out in the hall, just in time to see a footman carrying a note on a silver plate.

"This has just come for you, Mrs. Collins."

She took the note from the tray and thanked the servant. She returned to the sitting room, telling Jane that she'd received a note, which she opened.

"It is from a lawyer," said she. "He says I am needed to sign some sort of document related to William. He asks that, if possible, I go there this afternoon."

"I will come with you."

Elizabeth folded the note.

"Jane, it is in the city, and I will be there only to sign the document. There will be nothing for you to do, so I think I will go and get it over with."

"Are you sure? It's no trouble to go."

"You were out so long yesterday, you should stay in, in case there are any visitors. Aunt Gardiner will be here too. I shan't be any longer than I have to."

"Alright. You will go after we eat?"

"I will," and after the two ate with their aunt, Elizabeth found a hackney cab to take her to the old building off the Strand. Reaching the lawyer's office on the second floor—she never found out who the lawyer was—she was led into a room and found Darcy pacing.

Chapter 17. Mrs. Collins & Mr. Darcy Meet

After Mrs. Collins and Mr. Darcy exchanged courtesies, they sat on a pair of leather chairs at an angle to one another. Elizabeth declined Darcy's offer to have refreshments brought in, the more quickly to learn the news.

He granted her wish and began.

"I had an intimate dinner with Bingley last night. I decided not to beat about the bush. I asked him straight away. 'Jane Bennet,' I said. 'What are your thoughts about her?' He hardly seemed surprised. I think he has been pining to have someone simply bring up your sister's name.

"'I will tell you that I've never met her equal,' he said. 'I know it is unfair to those women I do meet, but I cannot help but compare them to her and they are all found wanting to me. Some dramatically so.'

"I told him that I had been reminded of her by the most random of circumstances involving my lawyer and a new Mr. Collins who is to inherit the Bennet estate. During the conversation with the lawyer, I told him, I discovered that Miss Jane Bennet was not as yet married. I believe this was news to him and quite pleasant news at that. I told him nothing about our walk though I *suggested* that her reluctance to commit to another might well reflect a desire to possibly commit to him."

This all was quite what Elizabeth hoped for.

"I think that he is most definitely interested in visiting your sister again."

"From what you say, I believe he is. But why did he abandon her in the first place?"

Darcy got up and paced a moment before sitting again.

"I must tell you something of which I am not proud. It is something I feel bound to reveal concerning *my* conduct, though I doubt you will find it justified. I am not certain that I can now justify my conduct, but I believe it was properly done when it was done."

"Mr. Darcy. You are all a mystery suddenly."

"As I said, it concerns my own conduct, but it also concerns your sister."

"My sister? Jane?"

"Yes. When Charles Bingley and I were at Netherfield, I saw that he was having an increasing attachment to her. In my view, and after careful observation, I doubted the sincerity of *her* feelings towards *him*, if, indeed, she had any."

Elizabeth was stunned by this. The entire tenor of what had been pleasant turned. *What could he be meaning? What could he have done?*

"How dare you presume to know my sister's feelings, especially towards another man? And you! What do you know of love?" Her anger could not be separated from her tone.

"I will admit that at the time, I knew nothing, but I believe that has changed, though that is neither here nor there for I am speaking of some time ago. I was alerted to growing expectations concerning your sister and my friend."

"From whom?"

"From virtually everyone, especially from your mother and even Sir William Lucas. I was determined to judge from my own observations whether there was any true affection on your sister's part, as I knew there was on my friend's."

"And how were you qualified to *judge* such a thing?"

"Whether I was qualified or not, it was an obligation I believed I had to undertake for my friend. I became most observant of your sister in her dealings with him and, frankly, they seemed no more than a passing fancy to me, as women are wont to have."

"Again, sir, you cannot and did not know what you are speaking of. My sister is the dearest creature and very shy, but I assure you, sir, that her affection for Charles Bingley was quite genuine. A blind man would have seen it were he truly motivated by concern for his friend. But that too is neither here nor there. What did you do?"

"With his sisters—"

"'With his sisters'? What are they to do with it?"

"Please, ma'am, allow me to continue. We encouraged him to leave Netherfield and when he had done so, not to return. We believed that a separation would reveal the true state of his affection, or lack of affection, for your sister."

"And you left her abandoned, anticipating for weeks and weeks that he would return until she received a letter from Caroline Bingley announcing that he would not. And then her being in London and his failure to visit, which established in her, sadly and you concede wrongly, that in fact he had no affection for her as she did for him."

"It is this that I must further address. While my initial participation in the effort to have him stay away from Netherfield I believe was justified by my concern that your sister was attempting to entrap him, as your mother suggested she—."

"My mother? What is that to do with anything?" Elizabeth's voice, if anything, had gotten louder and more desperate.

"Your mother made it eminently clear again and again that she was determined to have Charles Bingley marry your sister. From the first moment I saw her at the Meryton Assembly, I knew that was her scheme, however justified it might have been given your family's...financial circumstances. No, Mrs. Collins, I was convinced that your sister was, either voluntarily or not, a pawn in your mother's game. As I look back in these recent days I have come—"

"I assure you, sir, that Jane is not a pawn in anyone's game. She was, I thought after Mr. Bingley abandoned her, greatly his superior."

"It is in that respect that I must take full responsibility."

"I do not understand."

"In a way, Bingley was a pawn in *my* game."

"I do not understand." Elizabeth's anger was turning into utter confusion.

"I made sure that he did not know your sister was in town."

"He did not know Jane was with my uncle? After Jane visited his sisters and they returned the visit? He never knew?"

"That is it. *I* was aware but with his sisters we agreed that we would not admit to any knowledge of her being in town. We doubted very much that he would come across her in the places they frequented, and he did not. It is this that I believe was wrong of me, to not be forthcoming to my friend."

"To *lie* to your friend? What about what you did to Jane, let alone to Bingley, though your treatment of him makes me doubt that you are truly his friend."

"I suffer well enough, ma'am, from that suspicion. I tell you this because I realise the depth of affection they have for each other, however limited were their encounters in Hertfordshire. I have been an observer of Charles since leaving Netherfield and his abysmal efforts at having a connection with any woman are barely any efforts at all. And when I learned that your sister, too, remained unmarried, I realised that I was wrong there as well.

"So I have done, and will continue to do, what I can to facilitate their connection. It cannot atone, I know, for what I did, but I hope it will allow them to have happiness in the future."

A range of feelings flooded through her, but she forced herself to control them for the important information that he'd provided her. She sat deeper into her chair, and he returned to the one beside it.

"So, you see, it was not my friend's disinclination as to your sister that caused him to, as you say, abandon her. It was the legitimate—"

"*Legitimate?*"

"They were, I assure you, what at the time I truly believed were legitimate concerns of me and his sisters that he not himself be abandoned when he'd committed himself to her, as he was very wont to do. That he not be used as so many naïve men have been."

"And as he surely would have committed to her and allowed himself to love her had you not interfered. I will never understand why you and those women were so certain of your view about my sister that you decided to strip both her and, I believe, Charles Bingley of the rare chance one has in our sphere to be happy.

"I cannot say to you, sir, how harsh it is for someone to marry out of necessity and not out of love. To know she is throwing herself away because she had no choice but to do so. And for you and those others to do that to Mr. Bingley let alone to my sister is unforgiveable."

Elizabeth stood, preparing to leave. He got up and deftly placed himself between her and the office door.

"Mrs. Collins. I realise that what I have done will have caused me to have lost whatever good opinion you may have had of me forever. That cannot be helped, much as I regret it. But now, neither of us has the luxury of in a way abandoning the two who are of the greatest interest in this. We must come up with a scheme that will have the greatest chance of succeeding in bringing those two people, who you have convinced me would surely be happy together and surely would have been happy together had I not interfered, together."

To hasten Elizabeth's twin aims of aiding Jane with Bingley and seeing Fitzwilliam Darcy as infrequently as possible in the future, she resumed her seat. He remained standing.

"What do you have to suggest?" she asked.

And hard as it was for her to remain with this man after his confession, Elizabeth managed it and they agreed upon a course of action.

Chapter 18. The Arrangement

On the next day but one, Elizabeth insisted that Jane share a walk with her to the familiar area around St. Paul's, it being quite a fine day all around. Shortly before the cathedral's bells tolled noon, Elizabeth led her sister into a fine milliner's shop that overlooked the square to the south of the cathedral. She stood near the front window while Jane wandered throughout the shop.

"I'm sure you'll find something," Elizabeth said several times as she pretended to inspect hats and assorted bows and ribbons near the front window. Her attitude changed abruptly perhaps five minutes after they went in.

"I think we must go," she called as she put down a hat and Jane restored the bonnet she was examining onto its shelf. The pair were quickly on the pavement. Pretending to find something of interest in the window of the neighbouring shop, Elizabeth stopped.

It happened that two or three doors to the east of the milliner's there was supposed to be a fine gun shop, or so Darcy told his friend. He'd recently received word, he said, that a capital gun, a second size double-barrel one, had arrived. It was of the sort Bingley had enjoyed from Darcy's collection at Pemberley. Bingley might, said Darcy, quite like to have one of his own for when they next went to the country. But, Darcy regretted, he couldn't make it and it would be a shame for the gun to be sold before Bingley at least had a chance to inspect the weapon.

"Well, Darcy, I don't think I have any pressing engagements so I will visit it tomorrow."

"I suggest midday," Darcy had said. "Midday it shall be," agreed Bingley.

This exchange took place the evening before and now Bingley was on the pavement staring at where the gun shop was supposed to be. It was not there. *I must have mistranscribed the address,* he decided. Since Darcy made clear it was across from the main entrance to St. Paul's, he began to move from store to store until he came upon...Miss Jane Bennet, next to her sister and looking at displays in store windows. He froze. She finally glanced in his direction. The shock, for both, could not have been greater had a shot been fired in their direction from the sought-after gun itself.

Their eyes met. The connection, *their* connection, was immediate. Bingley hurried to her, dodging the other window gazers who stood between them.

"I cannot believe it! It is my dear Miss Jane Bennet herself. Can it possibly be?"

"Oh my God. Mr. Bingley. Is it you?"

The ensuing words and motions between the two were all a bit of a muddle, and Elizabeth stood where Jane had been, observing love resume its natural course, cleared of the wrongly placed dam that had blocked it. She stepped to them and suggested that a turn around the square in the front of the cathedral might be in order. Bingley, of course, forgot entirely about the gun he'd traveled to see (but that wasn't there) and insisted that he accompany the ladies back to the Gardiners' house and the three (mostly just the two) spoke little but nonsense the entire way. As they were about to separate, Bingley wrangled a promise from them that they would visit him and his dear sister Caroline at his house at No. 19, Mount Row in Bloomsbury the very next afternoon.

"Rain or shine, you will come, yes?" he asked in departing, receiving a "we promise to be there" from Elizabeth.

The night at the Gardiners' was somewhat awkward for another guest, however. Archibald Collins found the encouragement of just days before from Jane seemed to have evaporated. It was only during the course of the conversation that Mr. Gardiner let slip—he not having been cautioned to exercise discretion in the matter—that his nieces had the pleasure of meeting a fine gentleman, one they knew from when he rented an estate not three miles from Longbourn itself.

"You will come to know it well with your visits there, I am sure, Mr. Collins. It is Netherfield, isn't that right, Lizzy?"

Elizabeth said it was and that it was a fine house. She hoped that that would be sufficient to satisfy Mr. Collins's curiosity. It was not. It did not take long for the lawyer, being a clever enough fellow, to appreciate that something dramatic had happened since his last visit and it likely had to do with the gentleman who'd rented the estate not three miles from Longbourn itself.

But neither Jane nor Elizabeth was as unguarded as was their uncle. To Mr. Collins's thrusts towards them as to this gentleman—"a distant, passing friend perhaps?" Collins suggested—they parried them away with vagueness he could not puncture, and he left the house quite dissatisfied with the results of his visit.

Later, when they were alone in their room, Jane said to Elizabeth, "I cannot imagine it would be right to have Mr. Collins view things in a positive direction since there is a reason to think that any hopes he has about me will be disappointed."

She was on the little bench brushing her hair. Elizabeth sat in a small armchair that was placed in a corner for the purpose of keeping an eye over whomever sat on the bench.

"Oh, Jane. You are too good," her sister said. "I am not suggesting that you deceive Mr. Collins in any way. But there is much we do not know of him. About his true character. I think it best if for you to refrain from giving Mr. Collins any sort of or at least too much encouragement, at least till you have a better sense of what Mr. Bingley truly thinks of you—"

"Oh, Lizzy. His eyes and his words and his entire manner make clear the near equality of feelings we still have for one another, just from this one, fortuitous meeting. But I agree that I should allow it some time to see how it develops." She looked from the looking glass to her sister, the latter fighting the urge to contradict her sister's use of the word "fortuitous."

"I believe that a week should suffice."

How Elizabeth laughed at this silliness from her sister, which had become an all too rare occurrence.

"I would say a fortnight," Elizabeth countered, and neither could speak for laughing for some time and the concerns for Mr. Collins's feelings vanished as the two prepared for bed.

* * * *

CAROLINE BINGLEY WAS LIVID. She'd been told by her brother that the Bennet sisters—the Bennet sisters!—had been invited to visit and that as the lady of the house she was to see that they were treated properly. It was not enough, she seethed, that her brother told her of the chance meeting with these women.

Caroline Bingley knew nothing about what happened to Jane Bennet once she, and Darcy, had extricated her brother from what plainly would have been a most improvident match. She'd never regretted keeping Jane's presence in London from her brother and she wasted not a thought to what had become of her and her grasping mother and awful sisters.

Caroline Bingley knew her brother still pined for the pretty country bumpkin, and it was taking far longer than she expected for him to turn his attention to a more suitable match. He was, though, still young and healthy. Caroline had no doubt that he would succeed once he finally turned his mind to it. And now this!

Caroline Bingley was livid perhaps even more at Darcy. He'd given every assurance that he was to marry his cousin Anne de Bourgh after making it sufficiently and painfully clear that he would not be marrying Miss Caroline Bingley.

No.

Caroline Bingley wasn't fooled by the chance meeting in a place her brother would never have appeared but for being misled to go there. Only Darcy could have arranged it, and he orchestrated it, without doubt in coordination with the Collins widow, whom she never liked.

Caroline Bingley had heard about the death of poor Mr. Collins though she could not recall how. She knew nothing about Jane Bennet and imagined her mother had managed to marry her off despite her bad connections and worse relations. She did acknowledge, though, that the sweet Jane Bennet did possess an uncommon beauty even if she was a bit stupid, or at least vacant, unlike that sister of hers.

And how did Mrs. Collins find herself conspiring with Darcy? There was something different about Darcy since news of Mr.

Collins's demise reached town. Elizabeth Bennet or Collins or whatever her name was surely played a role in that change.

But notwithstanding these legitimate objections, the Bennets traveled together to the Bingleys on Mount Row. There was some awkward sitting and chatting in the fine house's drawing room until it was finally over and the Bennets, as Caroline Bingley would later tell her fortunate sister, finally returned to Cheapside.

Chapter 19. Mr. Collins's Misery

Mr. Archibald Collins was not long in his suffering. On his visit to the Gardiners' house on the ensuing Saturday, he requested the honour of accompanying them, and particularly the eldest Bennet, to services the next day. Mr. Gardiner, alas, had to disappoint those hopes. "I fear, sir, that we have already committed to be accompanied by another gentleman who has consented to have supper with us afterwards. I'm very sorry."

Archibald Collins was taken aback even more when Elizabeth said that the gentleman was the one earlier mentioned, the one who'd rented the estate three miles from Longbourn itself.

"Another time, I'm sure," he said with more than a little disappointment.

"You can count on that, sir," Mr. Gardiner added. "Count on it, indeed."

In fact, however, had Mr. Collins counted on it, he would have been made poorer by the exercise. He never did accompany Miss Bennet to St. Paul's for services on a Sunday. He stopped but irregularly at Gracechurch Street and then found himself relegated to nothing more than a distant relation with a future interest in Longbourn and not as a potential suitor for either eligible Bennet.

Any doubt was erased as to the senior Miss Bennet when Charles Bingley in a quite nervous and inconsistent—but not inconstant—voice made his great request to that lady in the front parlour of the Gardiners' house on Gracechurch Street and that lady wasted no time in accepting Charles Bingley's offer. It was on the Saturday next that Mr. and Mrs. Gardiner, Jane Bennet, and Mrs. Collins rode in a carriage and Charles Bingley rode on a horse the twenty or so miles to Longbourn. There, after the briefest of meetings between Bingley and Mr. Bennet, the consent to the marriage was obtained (as a matter of courtesy and not the law). Joy quickly spread through the house and in no time through the neighbourhood.

Mr. Bennet's consent was fully endorsed by Mrs. Bennet and it was decided that Jane Bennet and Charles Bingley would be wed at the old and rather fine church in Meryton—which the Bingleys had attended when they were at Netherfield—and wed there they were within a month's time.

We must pause this joyful recitation to observe that some of the guests at the wedding were not as enthused as they might otherwise have been. We speak in particular of Mrs. Louisa Hurst and Miss Caroline Bingley. A third person who'd conspired against the joining of the two, however, more than made up for it and was pleased in the (not insignificant) part he played in bringing the union about.

Bingley's great friend, Fitzwilliam Darcy, could hardly hide his role in sending Bingley in search of a capital gun at an imaginary gun shop across from the cathedral, and he confessed to his charade to Bingley that very evening of the "fortuitous" reunion.

"I'd never have thought you a romantic," Bingley had said in Darcy's library. "Sending me to Cheapside to look at a gun 'lest it be gone in the morning' indeed."

With a little prodding, Darcy explained why he had conspired to deny Bingley the knowledge that Jane Bennet was in Cheapside the prior year.

"Your complete lack of interest in any other woman forced me to reconsider my view more recently, Charles, and upon that and with a word with Mrs. Collins—"

"Wait. How does Lizzy Bennet, I mean Mrs. Collins, fit into this?"

He duly explained how Mrs. Collins fit into it and particularly how her assurance that her sister was still plainly in love with his friend and was plainly never likely to fall out of it, even with the threat of a new, attractive suitor waiting in the wings, was too compelling to be ignored.

"When I met him, this new Mr. Collins, I knew he was nothing like you but, as lawyers will, he was the sort of man who would be able to pretend to be something he was not."

"Darcy, I should never have forgiven you had you failed to protect Miss Bennet from him, even were I to have nothing to do with her."

Darcy knew his friend meant this.

"I cannot say whether I would have taken steps towards any other woman. But I would not for all the world have allowed anything averse to happen to someone you esteem so highly—"

"And who, I pray, you will come to esteem highly, too."

"I do hope so. As I say, I felt it was my obligation to protect her from who I am led to believe is truly a libertine and what has happened since has more than paid a thousand-fold for my efforts."

Darcy rose and collected a decanter of claret from a sideboard that night Darcy had made his confession and used it to fill both their glasses. When he resumed his seat, Bingley said, "And what of her sister? I always felt there was something...peculiar I might say, between you and Miss Elizabeth, as is the widow Mrs. Collins now."

Darcy delayed responding with a deep inhalation of the wine.

"Charles, I truly wish I knew. I truly do. It has caused me yet again to defer deciding about my cousin Anne."

"I only ask, then, that when you do discover it, you at least tell me. I should very much like you to have some portion of the joy that I currently have for seeing my angel Jane again."

Darcy smiled to his glass. *Yes, if I can only discover it.* To his friend, he said, "I should think the slightest portion of your joy would be more than sufficient for any man and it would surely be sufficient for a hard man like me. I promise you that you will learn of whatever feelings I have for Mrs. Collins once I have learned them myself."

But in the following weeks, as preparations were being made for the wedding, Darcy was no closer to having an answer to this riddle or puzzle than he was that evening in his library with Bingley or for that matter that earlier one with his cousin, Colonel Fitzwilliam. He often particularly wished he had the certainty about Elizabeth that Bingley had about her sister Jane.

He'd not seen Elizabeth—who confessed to that sister her role in the fateful charade across from St. Paul's the evening when Bingley proposed—until the very morning of the wedding. She was in half-mourning and had not visited while in town. Bingley was often at the Gardiners', but Darcy did not believe it appropriate that he accompany his friend.

Chapter 20. Darcy Speaks to Elizabeth

Though she was torn on the matter, Elizabeth did not think it appropriate for a sister, even if only in half-mourning, to actively participate in the wedding ceremony of Jane and Bingley as she otherwise surely would have. She instead sat on the far side of her parents throughout the ceremony while Kitty stood beside Jane.

Her eyes often strayed to Darcy, the groomsman, standing beside his great friend throughout. She watched as he and Kitty followed the new husband and the new wife down the aisle and out into the churchyard where a sizeable portion of the neighbourhood waited to congratulate the favourite of the Bennet girls on her great fortune in marrying such a kind (and wealthy) gentleman.

Elizabeth was not a witness to this. She'd slipped out through a side door to return alone to Longbourn. She was (she would admit if asked) quite satisfied on the turn of affairs for both Jane and Charles Bingley, who she—Elizabeth—quite liked and admired, especially for the certainty of his love for Jane.

She was nearly to the house when she heard, "Mrs. Collins."

The voice's source was himself soon upon her.

"I am sorry you will not be participating further in the festivities."

"Mr. Darcy, sir," she said with a curtsey, which he answered with a formal but slight bow. "I believe," she resumed, "circumstances dictate the extent to which I may participate much as I would like to have done more."

Mr. Darcy pointed with his arm ahead of himself, and the two resumed walking, at some slight distance from one another.

"If I may be so bold, and appropriate, I must congratulate you on the role you played in bringing them together."

"After the role *you* played in keeping them apart, you mean?"

She felt a moment of regret for again being sharper and less considerate of the feelings of this man than she was with anyone else of her acquaintance, and he again took a moment to recover.

"You are right to chastise me. I will tell you that I have frequently done the same in recent days, but I think we can both agree that it is quite good that they are now Mr. and Mrs. Charles Bingley."

"On that at least we can agree."

He began to respond, to express the futility of seeking forgiveness, when they'd reached the gravel drive in front of the house and stopped to face each other.

"I believe," she said, "that you have obligations elsewhere and I should not wish to keep you from them."

Is this to be my fate? he thought as he mouthed, "You are correct. I had best be returning."

He bowed and she curtseyed.

"If I can be of any future service to you, Mrs. Collins, please seek me out, if you will, and I will endeavour to be at your service."

He bowed again and she turned and went inside the empty house. Though not before stealing a glance back at him, as he again was walking away from her.

Chapter 21. Elizabeth's Journey to Brighton

Under normal circumstances, Elizabeth would have accompanied her sister on the trip the Bingleys were taking to the Lake District, which would be followed by a month as guests at Pemberley.

There was still over a month, though, before Elizabeth would be free of her mourning obligations. With the married Jane off on her wedding trip and beginning her new life and up in the north of England, she decided to accompany Kitty and Lydia to Brighton for an extended stay. Each of her officer brothers-in-law had received leases from their fathers to one of a pair of fine adjoining houses some blocks north of the pier and well away from the tumult and unpleasantness of the camp itself and the streets nearby where many a woman and girl (and even very discreetly boy) plied their trade for the lonely and many a tavern provided refreshment for thirsty soldiers.

No, the Denny and Pratt lodgings were well away from that. Indeed, the two houses were near a small green that was well treed and had several walks and benches spread about. It was a quite popular place for walking or even promenading on a fine day.

For her part, Elizabeth relished the idea of spending time by and perhaps even *in* the sea after the very long period of being landbound.

The day after the wedding, a carriage transported Jane and Charles—Mr. and Mrs.—Bingley with Darcy to the north. A second carrying Elizabeth, Kitty, and Lydia headed south, while Denny and Pratt escorted them on horseback.

Unlike the prior day, this one was somewhat blustery and did not clear until those going to Brighton reached London, where they stopped for a fine meal at a tavern. And by nightfall they'd arrived, and Elizabeth was established in her room at the Pratts'.

On her first afternoons there, she went out with Kitty and Lydia around the town and along the pier with the occasional visit to Mrs. Forster and other militiamen's wives, excepting the one when it rained and rained for the entirety of the daylight hours. Bathing huts lined the beach, and many men and women were in the water on several days. But Elizabeth was able to convince her sisters that she was not yet ready to herself plunge in. Instead, she was happy to sit on a bench on the promenade, watching Kitty and Lydia being Kitty and Lydia on the beach and in the Channel.

After being in Brighton for nearly a week, Elizabeth begged to be allowed to stay in while her sisters were off doing their visits. When they were gone, she made herself comfortable in the Pratts' front parlour. It was not a large room. That was among its attractions. She sank into a chair by a window that looked out at the street where she could interrupt her reading with glances out at the passing people and horses and carriages.

It was delightfully calming to her, to feel part of a city, a something she'd never felt at Longbourn or Hunsford, for all their tranquility. She had a recent novel she'd fallen into and was well into it when she heard the bell. She'd not noticed anyone coming up the short path to the door, but in a moment heard that door opened, and an inquiry made by the Pratts' manservant. This was followed promptly by a knock on the parlour's door.

"Begging your pardon, Mrs. Collins," Davis said after he came in, "But there is a gentleman here to see you. It is a Mr. George Wickham, ma'am."

Elizabeth was immediately on her feet, her book tossed onto the seat as she was vacating it.

"Show him in, Davis, show him in."

And in he was shown, as she was trying to make herself at least somewhat presentable to the former officer and now widower.

Elizabeth had learned what became of Wickham when Kitty and Lydia brought their fiancés to Longbourn. How he'd married a woman he met at an officers' ball. How she was the well-off daughter of an estate holder outside of Crawley, a town to the north of Brighton. How she had a small but not inconsiderable fortune from her mother's side and had fallen quickly (and deeply) for the officer and unlike what happened with Miss King (whose uncle snatched her away, permanently, to Liverpool when they (and her ten thousand) were nearly to the altar) they were soon married.

He was able, Lydia told Elizabeth in a whisper, to clear his sizeable gambling debts and promised to give up that particular vice as a condition of the marriage, a condition that his future father-in-law was able to secure with certain restrictions on the deed for the parcel on the estate that became his daughter's and thus his son-in-law's upon the marriage. Alas, a sudden fever took and overwhelmed her, and she was dead not four months after the wedding.

"He's now, Denny tells me, something of a gentleman farmer with a smallish house on the estate. He comes to our balls and dinners now that he is out of mourning," Lydia had said, "and" (again in a whisper) "as presentable and handsome as ever, Lizzy."

Oh, how Lydia and Kitty laughed at that.

And now here he was. The well-off widower, Elizabeth saw, quite as presentable and handsome as ever, though with a few more wrinkles surrounding his eyes and a few more pounds surrounding his middle.

"Mrs. Collins," he now said to her when they were a suitable distance to exchange courtesies, "I must tell you how pained I was to have heard of the tragedy that befell you with your husband's death."

"Thank you, sir. It was nearly a year, and of course I must express to you my deep condolences for your own loss."

"You have heard, then?"

"Indeed. The sad news was given to me when my sisters visited me at Longbourn."

"Yes, I imagine it would have, from your delightful sisters."

She nearly stepped even closer to him before catching herself.

"I was just reading." She nodded at the novel on the chair.

"So, I can see. I do not wish to intrude."

"Mr. Wickham. I can assure you, your presence is no intrusion. May I get you some refreshment?"

"Indeed, not, Mrs. Collins. But—" (and he looked out the window) "seeing how it is in fact a quite fine day and you are cloistered here—I mean no disrespect for what I am sure in the fine volume you are reading" (and he nodded to the book) "but I would very much like to have a turn with you about the nearby green."

"Mr. Wickham. Nothing could give me greater pleasure."

After she'd exchanged her white cap for a bonnet with a purple strip and put a violet shawl over her shoulders, the two were soon on the path that encircled the green. There were two or three people who recognised her even in the short period since she'd arrived, and they nodded in sympathy to her and smiled at how well she appeared to have recovered herself with the very fine man beside her.

"I will confess, Mrs. Collins, that there have been occasions when my thoughts drifted to the pleasant times we had together when I was at Meryton."

"They were pleasant, weren't they?"

"Among the pleasantest I have ever known. Even with my dear wife. I loved her greatly, of course, but in many respects, she was not your equal."

"We each had our obligations and necessities to consider and…and it appeared that those and fate would cause us to be separated forever."

"Did you not think of me at all?"

"I confess to you, Mr. Wickham, that I did sometimes have thoughts of you."

Her thoughts at times ventured to how things might have been different. They ventured at times in a (physical) direction about which she sometimes felt guilty afterward. George Wickham had nothing. She wondered, though, what life might have been for her as a clergyman's wife, or at least a clergyman with whom she could experience a passion of the sort she never knew or could even imagine with her own Mr. Collins.

Now, as they walked in Brighton, she was nearly transported back to the many happy strolls they took in and around Meryton. How he told her that much as he enjoyed the soldier's life, he would have preferred to have had what was so cruelly and unfairly taken from him by Fitzwilliam Darcy, the master of Pemberley.

"My prospects of becoming a clergyman are long since passed, as you well know."

"Of course, had you been a clergyman, I should never have become acquainted with you, and I would not surrender that small pleasure for all the world."

"Small, perhaps, to you, Mrs. Collins, but hardly that for me. I would not surrender it for the world."

"Do not take offense, sir. That I can recall them so well and so fondly proves their importance to me."

They came upon a bench from which a couple had just arisen, and he led her to it. They were both careful about how they looked to those passing the gentleman with the half-mourning lady. Her hands were in her lap and his were in his and they kept a suitable (or nearly suitable) distance from one another.

The conversation drifted into descriptions of what life had held for them since they last met, and their talk came naturally until Wickham felt it was time for her to return to the house and for him to arrange another time when he could visit.

"Perhaps the six of us, the comrades in arms and the Bennet sisters, can undertake some type of outing for an afternoon, subject to the restraints that you are under, Mrs. Collins."

As they reached the house, Elizabeth promised that she would consult with her sisters about such a suggestion.

"I understand congratulations are in order for your elder sister having forfeited the 'Miss Bennet' that she long carried."

"Indeed. That is now gone from our family, she being the last to marry among us. How did you?...Lydia."

"Well, not directly. I paid a visit to the barracks yesterday and good Denny could not wait to provide me with the news."

"And that I had come to Brighton?"

"I will confess that that bit of intelligence might have been passed on to me."

This led them both to share the knowing laugh of the type they fell into when they'd first met and often walked—as they now walked—as dear friends.

"And I'm given to understand that my old nemesis Darcy was at the proceedings."

The very name and her companion's reminder of the injustice done to him when he would not give Wickham the living he'd been promised by Darcy, Sr. were jarring but she recovered. "He was, but I said scarcely a word, given my current situation. I will say he was polite and no more and I daresay he gave little real thought to me and even less to you."

"If he thought of me at all, which I greatly doubt."

"Now, Mr. Wickham. Let us put any thoughts of that disagreeable man aside and speak of an infinitely more pleasant one." (And Darcy did seem disagreeable to her, when he was in the presence of this particular gentleman.)

"What could you mean, Mrs. Collins?"

"I mean you, of course, if I may be so forward."

* * * *

KITTY AND LYDIA WERE beyond excited on learning from Elizabeth herself that Mr. George Wickham had visited and that he and Elizabeth took a turn around the green. Their husbands were less impressed. At dinner, the conversation quickly turned to their erstwhile colleague.

"He was greatly missed when he went off to marry that pot of money," Lydia said, "though it was something of a blessing since it allowed me to focus on the far more promising presence of a certain Lieutenant Peter Denny."

"Well," said Kitty. "She was very plain, and I suppose rich enough..."

"And he was in quite dire economic straits," Denny interrupted only to be interrupted in turn by Pratt: "And beggars cannot be choosers, you know."

Elizabeth well knew that but kept silent. Lydia did not. With a huff, she resumed the floor. "In any case, yes, Lizzy, I do believe most of his fellow officers were glad that he was taken as they did not much care to be competing with him for ladies' attentions."

"Or *affections*," Kitty added before the pair of them briefly laughed until they recovered themselves in light of the circumstances in which they were telling the story.

"She was rich enough to seduce him, and he and his bride moved into a house on her father's small estate," Lydia said, "but tragically it all came crashing down when she died so horribly."

"And he has her money and her house and has apparently become quite the gentleman."

"And he comes to visit us—"

"More our husbands," Kitty said.

"I think he's happy that we are there too, Kitty," Lydia added. "So, we have seen him at least once a month since that tragedy, and especially when the year was up."

"And when was that?" Elizabeth asked.

"It was, I think, about two months ago. He is a regular visitor now to Brighton. To us and to other officers."

"With all his supposed charms," Pratt added with a laugh.

Chapter 22. Elizabeth Writes to Jane

Awaiting Mrs. Bingley's arrival at Pemberley from the Lake District was a letter, leaning squarely against a mirror over a chest of drawers in the lavish bedchamber that had been assigned to her.

Dear Mrs. Bingley,

I could not resist calling you so, but you shall always be my 'Dearest Jane.' I hope that your trip with Charles to the Lake District has been what you hoped it would be and you have seen at least some of it when you are able to turn your eyes from your dear husband.

I do not know when you arrive at Pemberley—where I am led to believe there is at least one fine lake not far from the great house—and are able to read this so I cannot know how stale my news will be and whether it will have been overtaken by events.

What news? you ask. It is simply that I have resumed a high degree of cordiality with George Wickham. He is a widower, as I am sure you were informed by Kitty and Lydia when you saw them. He still deeply mourns the loss of his wife but when he arrived to console me for my loss, I found that I could be of service to him with respect to his own.

I daresay that once my period of mourning for my late Mr. Collins is ended in less than a month, the feelings that I have for Mr. Wickham, which I believe to be to some extent reciprocated, may have the opportunity to flower.

Because of such news, I find myself unready and unwilling to speak of the more mundane events of my visit here. Kitty and Lydia are quite well, and each is endeavouring to become with child before the other, which would be amusing were it not such a serious bit of business.

Perhaps I will have more to tell you about them when I next write. I expect that you will write to me now and tell me of how wonderful your husband is, and, in anticipation of your assertions in that regard, I assure you that I have every confidence in the absolute correctness about anything you have to say about him.

I wish you and him (and your Derbyshire host) the best of health and hope to see you again when you return to town.

Lizzy

* * * *

ELIZABETH'S ENTHUSIASM for Wickham did not wane in the succeeding weeks. Indeed, it appeared to push aside her deep yet muddled thoughts of Darcy and the feelings she uncovered and wrote (only to herself in the end) about while she was in Hunsford, which she did not dare mention in this letter. Her own confusion about her...heart was, if anything, enhanced as the handsome widower again proved himself a gentleman of charm and grace and now some funds.

In Brighton, Mrs. Collins and Mr. Wickham walked often, and he took her to visit his in-laws at his wife's family's estate in Crawley. While there, he gave her a tour of the small house, not much larger in fact than the Hunsford Parsonage, that he had shared with his wife.

Yes, thought Elizabeth, *I could be very content here.*

This mood was overturned and quite abused, however, when she had an unexpected and not particularly welcome visitor at Kitty's several days after touring Wickham's house and some weeks after her reintroduction to the widower. She'd just come in after leaving him on the pavement in front of the Pratts' house and was already in her room getting comfortable when she heard the bell.

There was shortly a knock on her door and the manservant opened it when invited to and after a glance at a card said, "It's a Mr. Darcy, ma'am, looking quite impatient, if I must say."

This was horribly inconvenient as well as distasteful and shocking, but Elizabeth felt obliged to see him and said she would be down. *What was the great Mr. Darcy doing in her sister's house in Brighton?* They'd had no communication since that afternoon of Jane's wedding when they spoke and walked briefly. She hoped it was about Jane since the alternative, that it concerned *her*, quickly set her stomach adrift.

Sooner begun, sooner ended.

When she reached the front parlour and allowed herself a deep breath before opening and then closing the door behind her, she exchanged greetings with him. It took several moments but she was able to recover her equilibrium from that first sight of him, standing quite formally yet quite naturally, as was his wont. Indeed, here, too, his manner was worlds apart from that of the gentleman she'd only recently walked with.

Now it was he who took a deep breath as she waited for him to say to her what he'd come so far to say.

"Pardon the intrusion, Mrs. Collins. I come on a matter of great significance, and I hope that I may be of some service to you. In this instance, it is *not* about your sister."

"Please sit, Mr. Darcy," she instructed, coldly, her mind racing as to what else it could possibly be about. The pair settled into armchairs separated by a small, rectangular table. "I truly cannot imagine what further service you can provide me, sir."

"I have been led to understand that you have renewed your acquaintance with George Wickham."

"From my sister, of course. I wish I had enjoined her from speaking of it. Still, I cannot see how that is any of *your* business, beyond coming to beg my forgiveness for what you did, or did not do, for him regarding the living your father promised was his."

Darcy was briefly undone. He had not anticipated this line of attack from the widow.

After a slight pause, he said, perhaps more coldly than *he* expected, "I hope to be able to provide you with my justification for making this my business and venturing so far to see you, if you will allow me."

She nodded. "Go on."

He stood.

"I have come to know and admire you in many respects and I believe it incumbent upon me to provide information of which I am personally aware and to which I can personally vouch concerning certain aspects of the life of George Wickham. You may choose to disregard what I say. That is, of course, your prerogative. But I pray that you do not and at least do *me* the courtesy of allowing me to continue."

"I at least owe you the courtesy of having you say what you wish to say to me," Elizabeth replied.

"Thank you." He gave her a slight nod.

"You will likely recall the coldness you witnessed when I came upon him with you and your sisters and Mr. Collins when Wickham first appeared in Meryton."

"I recall it quite well."

"Indeed." He resumed his pacing. "As I believe you know, George Wickham was the son of the steward of Pemberley."

"Yes, he disclosed that to me soon after we met."

"Yes. He may have told you, and it is true, that he was much loved by my father. Indeed, I daresay that in some respects my father wished his own son was more like the son of his caretaker. He was my father's godson and my father treated him at times almost as if he were his own son.

"I concede that my father in any case greatly admired the boy. He was a playmate of mine, and we spent many an hour romping around the Pemberley Woods and running to Lambton when we were old enough to do so. We would race the final yards. The two of us straining when we were twelve or thirteen was a frequent sight in that town. He would laugh that we should allow betting on the contest so we could make some money from our efforts.

"And how we'd laugh as we returned all sweaty and happy in the carriage his father sent to collect us. At that and at so many other things as boys of comparable ages and locations, if not in circumstances, will."

"It sounds ideal for you both," Elizabeth interrupted, still keeping a careful watch on the narrator's face as he, the narrator, crossed back-and-forth in front of her. "You in your exposure to him and him in his exposure to you. What changed?"

"I do not know that anything *changed*. I think we both started to grow into men and some of the character that the world finds appropriate in a boy may not be so acceptable in a man."

He resumed a seat beside her.

"I will not say that I was a perfect boy and that I grew into a perfect man. Far from it. I believe, however, that I have done a better job of it than did George Wickham."

"But circumstances," interrupted Elizabeth. "What can you tell me of what he actually did that brings you all this way to warn me from him?"

"I did not say my attempt was to warn you from him?"

"Oh, sir. Do not treat me so nonobservant to doubt your purpose. But go on."

"I assure you, ma'am, that whatever my motive, and perhaps I was too naïve to think you would find it as...innocent as I represent it to be, what I will tell about George Wickham, the *circumstances* of George Wickham, are true.

"His father died some twelve years ago. My father's own death was five years later, my mother having been long since gone. She, Lady Anne, was. by the way, Lady Catherine's sister. Though he was not old, my father had prepared himself for what would happen when he did die and one specific thing he most wanted to have happen was that George Wickham would be provided for.

"In addition to giving him a legacy of one thousand pounds, my father extracted a promise from me that should he have died when a living I would control came available, it would be Wickham's. I graciously gave my consent, knowing of the relationship between him and my father. It was a good living in the village of Kympton, not very distant from Pemberley itself."

"But he did not get it."

"No. He did not get it."

"Because you would not allow it."

"Mrs. Collins. He did not get it because he did not want it."

"I don't understand."

"I was prepared to provide it to him without conditions when it became available. The incumbent was elderly. Wickham, too, would have enough income and accommodation at Pemberley until he could undertake the privilege of having the living. He had, after all, been educated at Cambridge with me, thanks to my father, so he could take orders and attempt to qualify himself with the bishop to become a clergyman.

"He decided he did not want it. Shortly after my father's death, Wickham told me his preference was to study the law. He asked that I immediately provide him with the value of the living. I will admit that I was relieved by his suggestion. I knew that he ought not to be a clergyman. The one thousand pounds would not be enough, he said, to sustain him in his legal studies. He asked what he would receive in lieu of the living. I felt it was fairly worth three thousand pounds, and he agreed.

"He received his four thousand pounds and left me. I did not like him by that point and so had no connection with him either at Pemberley or in town."

Elizabeth interrupted. "I do not know why your not liking him can matter. All he did was decide to become a lawyer and not a clergyman and I cannot see how that should affect *my* opinion of him."

"Insofar as he claims that I ignored my father's wishes in refusing him the living, the falsity of that accusation, as I have explained it was, surely reflects on his honesty and thus his character. I feel I must make it known to you. But there is more."

"I will listen calmly, sir, for whatever else you wish to say on the subject."

"Thank you. I turn now to something far more painful, to what happened between George Wickham and my family."

"Your *family*?"

"Mrs. Collins, it would hardly give me cause to condemn the man and to broadcast my view of him to the world, or at least to you, were what I told you all that happened and were there not additional, unfortunate things to be said about his conduct."

"In fairness to you, he did lead me to believe that you denied him the living your father wished him to have for no reason or simply for your jealousy as to your father's fondness for him."

"So, you see he has lied to you on that."

"If you are telling me the truth."

"I assure you; you will know that I have told you the truth about his surrendering the living when I tell you what I was reluctant to tell you but that I now see I must. And for these facts, I can refer you to my cousin Colonel Fitzwilliam, who I know will confirm the accuracy of what I tell you.

"As I said, the living was not available when my father died or when Wickham gave it up. That changed some three years after the transaction I just recited to you. That is when the incumbent of the living in Kympton died. I'd heard nothing from Wickham until he heard of the vacancy, at which time he wrote to me. He said things had gone badly for him in the meantime but that he had reconsidered and rejected the law as a most unprofitable study and wished very much to be ordained. Would I provide the living to him? There was no one else, he said, who I had selected, and he reminded me of my father's intentions.

"Under all the circumstances, particularly my knowledge of how unsuitable being a clergyman was for him, I declined his multiple entreaties."

"But it would have been so beneficial to him."

"Mrs. Collins, I appreciate your view but here, too, I assure you that my decision was the correct one as you will soon discover."

Elizabeth sat further back into her chair as he again rose.

"You have yet to meet my sister, Georgiana."

"She was mentioned by Mr. Wickham, and I believe by your aunt."

"Yes, I was with you in the latter circumstance. As you imply, Wickham well knew her. She is ten years my junior, and Colonel Fitzwilliam and I have been her guardians since my father died."

He resumed his seat and leaned towards Elizabeth, who duplicated the motion to get closer to him and allow him to lower his voice.

"After I refused his request—please, Mrs. Collins, allow me to continue—after I refused his request, he disappeared from my life. That is until about a year before you and I met in Meryton. Georgiana was in school and then taken from there to an establishment formed for her in London.

"There was a lady, a Mrs. Younge, who presided over the establishment. My cousin and I interviewed her and were satisfied with her testimonials, though, as you will see, we were deceived. She took Georgiana to Ramsgate, to the sea with my knowledge and consent. Unbeknownst to me or Colonel Fitzwilliam, lo and behold, George Wickham appeared there. I would learn later that he and Mrs. Younge had a prior acquaintance—the nature of which I need not tell you—and the pair of schemers set out to convince Georgiana to elope and become Mrs. George Wickham."

"Mr. Wickham has said she is a proud girl, not unlike yourself."

"My sister, I will acknowledge, has certain of my tendencies and may suffer for having lived so long without her mother, but, and you must admit a brother's right to speak well of his only living close relation, I find her growing into one with the sweetest of dispositions. More, I venture to say, like your sister, who is now Mrs. Bingley, than you."

"Let us hope she is more like Jane than me."

Elizabeth was shocked when she realised how easily she was again finding it had become to speak to the fearsome Fitzwilliam Darcy, particularly on such a delicate and obviously painful concern of his. And she hadn't realised that all of her initial anxiousness had vanished. He soon returned to the somber tone he'd assumed since leaning towards her.

"I happened to go to Ramsgate to visit my sister earlier than expected. It was shortly before the elopement was to take place. My appearance, you will guess, was not kindly taken by either Mr. Wickham or Mrs. Younge. Georgiana immediately told me of the entire plan and agreed to give up taking one further step with George Wickham, who immediately fled. Mrs. Younge was of course dismissed from having any future dealings with Georgiana. My sister was fifteen at the time."

"But why?"

"Why did Wickham want to elope with her? First, she had thirty thousand pounds, which would have done even someone like Wickham for some time. But beyond that was his getting his revenge on me."

Without realising it, Darcy's jaw tightened, and his gaze was no longer in the room.

"He would be so happy de—. Having her as his bride, thinking of how any intimacy between them would cut into my heart. He would drink and gamble and…do various other inappropriate things, and my sweet Georgiana would always be Mrs. George Wickham and I would be helpless to do anything about it."

His wandering thoughts returned to the room and to the woman he felt duty-bound to speak of this.

"You will not, I know, reveal this to anyone." His eyes, perhaps even more watery than were hers, struck her as being as unlike the Fitzwilliam Darcy she had met in Meryton as any pair of eyes could possibly be. The thought and the sight rendered her speechless till she was brought out of her daze by his standing, instantly reverting back to the man she generally thought he was.

"I have taken too much of your time, Mrs. Collins. I have spoken the truth to you about these events."

He stepped to a secretary and removed a sheet of stationery and a pen and inkwell. He scrawled a few lines and handed them, still wet, to her.

"Should you require corroboration, you may contact my cousin. You will not doubt, I know, his integrity and I will write to him assuring him that it was at my request that you contacted him. But it will take much time. He is doing his duty in America, but God willing that he is able, he will respond to any inquiries you make of him."

"Sir. Caroline Bingley made statements about Mr. Wickham to me. She said it as something of a warning."

"She did not know any details but must have heard about his being denied the living. It was nothing to do with Georgiana. As I said, very few know of that. I'm sure Wickham and Mrs. Younge never told anyone what they conspired to do. And Bingley does not know. I know you will maintain my confidences."

"Of course," she said.

Hearing that, he quickly bowed and turned and was gone. She rushed to the window and opened it.

He was just on the walk to the pavement.

"Mr. Darcy, sir. How can I contact you should the need arise?"

"I will be staying at the Sussex Arms for several days. I will be at your service should you wish to speak to me."

He gave her a bow and was gone for good. Elizabeth watched till she could see him no more and then plopped herself down on the chair in which she sat during his story—though she was in no doubt that it was the truth—and looked at the stern writing on the page he'd handed to her.

Col. Richard Fitzwilliam

xxxxxxxxx

She knew she wouldn't write to him. She knew there was no need. Whatever may be said or thought about Fitzwilliam Darcy, there was not a scintilla of doubt as to his integrity.

It followed, then, that there could be little doubt as to George Wickham's lack thereof.

Chapter 23. Mr. Darcy in Brighton

The interview with Mr. Darcy lasted for less than half an hour but to Elizabeth it seemed to have gone much more quickly.

When he was gone, she asked the manservant not to reveal that she'd had a visitor and went up to her bedchamber. There she sat quietly on a wooden chair from which she enjoyed looking out over the rear of the house to the backs of those on the next street over. She'd carried her book with her but paid it no mind and let it drop into her lap as she drifted to a quite pleasant place, that is until she was roused by the ruckus caused by the Pratts' return and Kitty bursting in with the most glancing of knocks. Elizabeth was (as she had been at the Gardiners') glad to have asked the manservant to refrain from mentioning the visit or particularly her visitor, and Kitty's first question was the innocent enough, "What have you been doing all afternoon?" parried with a "I read some and after a while came up here."

Kitty paraded around the room displaying some sort of scarf that she insisted was vastly superior to the "ghastly thing" on which Lydia had spent even more money and would not leave until Elizabeth expressed her deeply held view that it was "very nice."

The evening passed well. There were no additional visitors other than Mr. and Mrs. Denny and apart from yet another squabble between her sisters—in this case which of them got the better scarf at the better price—it proved a delightful night, ending after the four others played some hands of whist whilst Elizabeth did some needlepoint as a gift to Jane.

Things were less pleasant in the morning for it was then that Mr. George Wickham himself made an appearance. He'd come down from Crawley and would be accompanying the others into town for a nice afternoon bite at a rickety café overlooking the pier.

As was often the case, the married couples advanced while the non-married pair lapsed behind.

"You are awfully quiet, Mrs. Collins," Wickham observed after some minutes of silence.

"It is nothing, I think, but I am being on the edge of a headache with this sun."

It was a bright day and none of the ladies had brought a parasol and their bonnets did little to provide shielding.

"We must not take chances, ma'am. I will tell the others that we are going back to the Pratts'."

He started on that errand but turned.

"Do not be concerned," he said. "I will stay with you at the house until the others return."

He'd taken only a step or two when Elizabeth called him back.

"Oh, Mr. Wickham. I am dreadfully appreciative of your offer, but when I return, I think I must lie down. I know you have plans to be with your fellows and I wouldn't for a fortune wish to interfere with them. It will be enough for you to walk me back and you can quickly rejoin them. I hate to think I caused a second in our party to suffer from my delicate constitution."

And as they had not gone very far, within ten minutes Elizabeth was back at the Pratts' and Wickham had rejoined the others for the day.

Her sisters and brothers-in-law were back some hours later, during which Elizabeth attempted to read more of her novel, with scant success. Lydia said that Wickham regretted having to proceed directly to Crawley on some matter related to his father-in-law. This time, the group assembled at the Dennys' for dinner and cards. Elizabeth again declined playing the game but between deals she asked the men what *they* thought of Wickham.

"I knew there was something going on there, Lizzy." Lydia was delighted with the news and delighted that she'd long suspected it.

Elizabeth ignored her sister. "I am simply inquiring of someone who seems quite changed from when I met him."

"I will say that he has changed, don't you agree Pratt?" Denny began.

"Indeed, I do." He spoke as he dealt the cards. "Since he was married, he seems not nearly so *carefree* as he was when he first joined the militia."

"That is very true. I sometimes thought he joined not simply because of a need for employment to pay for his...his habits but also for some protection from a jealous husband."

The two men fell into laughing and Lydia entered the fray.

"Oh yes, Lizzy. When he was in Meryton, he was apparently quite quiet—"

"Resting, I daresay, from what he had done," Kitty said.

"And what he planned to do," Lydia added, and the four fell into apoplexy.

"He was very bad in Brighton when we arrived," Denny said. "Never in want of company as I recall."

Pratt added, "We were quite jealous, Denny and I, until we came to renew our friendships with your dear sisters, Mrs. Collins."

"You had better be," Lydia said with a mocking scold, after which the game proceeded, and the banter went in a different direction until after Pratt played in his turn. He then said to Elizabeth, "I have heard he wasn't always particular in his choice of...bedmates in size or age or standing and there were rumours in the regiment that he somewhat reverted to his old ways not long after his missus was gone."

"Thank you, lieutenant," Elizabeth said somewhat coldly and against the stream of joviality running through the parlour.

Rumours all, but how could they be doubted? Elizabeth tried to find a morsel of such roguishness in her own dealings with Wickham but could not think of any. And the matter was overtaken by others of more interest to the cardplayers while Elizabeth returned to her needlepoint.

In her room later, Elizabeth continued her internal struggle. It was clear to her. Wickham was guilty of what many men would consider a series of misdemeanors that they would laugh at and envy, yet many women would know them to be felonies. *Would she?*

She felt, though, that she owed the widower the chance to address the accusations made against him. The opportunity quickly presented itself. He was the Pratts' late the next morning and after greeting Elizabeth and Kitty, Elizabeth asked to speak with him. Alone. Kitty was of course more than willing to leave the two to speak of what she was sure they would speak of.

George Wickham likely shared that expectation. He was thrilled when Elizabeth offered to take a turn around the green again, and off they went, with Kitty watching them from an upstairs window as they stepped from the house.

When the couple reached the path, Elizabeth told Wickham that Darcy had come to see her. This news disconcerted him. Before he could react, though, she repeated what she'd been told. When she finished, he directed her to a bench.

"Mrs. Collins, it is me who is being defamed here. I know it's Darcy's continued effort to keep me from having *any* happiness. I am only glad that he could not interfere with my own marriage and my being left free to marry someone I loved."

His umbrage about whether he planned to elope with Georgiana was palpable. She had not wished to mention it, to breach her promise to Darcy, but could see no alternative.

"But do you deny that you considered going and marrying her, even without the consent of her brother and guardian?"

"I had every intention of obtaining his consent. He did not give us the chance. He was blinded by rage when he saw me, and he realised what I was to Georgiana. It was little of *my* doing. I did not force her to do *anything*. I happened to see her in London—or more, perhaps, she happened to see me—before she and Mrs. Younge went to Ramsgate. Mrs. Younge said Georgiana was miserable and pining for me."

"How did you know Mrs. Younge?"

"How did I know Mrs. Younge? I had met her in Lambton some years before. She is not a young lady, if you didn't know. She was kind to me when I was alone—"

"I am sure she was."

"What does that mean? She was no more than a friend to me, and I often spent a pleasant evening with her, and others too, while we were both in town after I left Derbyshire. If you think anything untoward happened between us, that is a slander on her character, and I will not stand for it."

Wickham rose and stood before Elizabeth, waiting.

"Let us resume our walk with quieter tempers," he suggested in a calmer tone. He extended his hand, which she took as she got up, and they began another turn around the green.

"I happened to be in the house where she acted as Georgiana's governess and I happened to be seen by Miss Darcy. I'd not thought of her for some time, and she was, of course, always simply a girl to me, on whom I confess I sometimes doted.

"So, when Mrs. Younge wrote to me in town that Miss Darcy, having quite by happenstance seen me, as I said, was lonely and missed her brother and Pemberley, I felt obligated to go see her."

"How did she know your address?"

"My address? I must have written it for her for one reason or another. It hardly matters, does it?"

Elizabeth kept her silence.

"In any event, she did write to me about Georgiana Darcy. She wanted me to help the poor girl's spirits. When I arrived, Georgiana made it clear that in her thoughts she was no longer a girl but a woman. She insisted that I accept her as a woman. As *my* woman.

"I need not say how shocked I was by this announcement. *She wished to be my wife.* It was a flattering suggestion by someone so young and, well, naïve, and I did no more than say I would consider it. More than anything, it was to keep her amused, expecting that she'd come to her senses in a day or two. In any event, I would seek her brother's consent, which I knew he would not give, and that would be that.

"So, I would not have married her. I just was searching for a means for her to realise that without having to break her heart."

"I will take you at your word. That Darcy and his cousin—"

"Colonel what's his name? The earl's son. Have you communicated with him?"

"It is Colonel Fitzwilliam and as he is fighting in America, I have not had the chance to communicate with him."

"I assume Darcy is grateful for that bit of geography."

"To the contrary. He has encouraged that I write."

"A message that would be months in arriving and for which any response would take months in returning. But the Colonel would know no more of these matters than would Darcy."

"There remains the other matter."

"Other matter?"

"You told me that Darcy refused to give you the living his father intended for you."

"And he did."

"But is it not the case that you endeavoured to enter the legal profession after the death of the elder Mr. Darcy?"

"That was just until the living became available. I needed to eat."

"I suppose. So, you did not surrender any rights you had to the living for three thousand pounds."

"Is that what he told you?"

"Is it true?"

"Initially, I admit, I was not as…enthusiastic about becoming a clergyman as I might once have been. But as the law did not ultimately appeal to me and as the living became available, I petitioned Darcy to have it be given to me. He outright refused. It is something for which I will never forgive him. I would have been content in such a position."

"But you gave it up."

"I admit that, yes, I did."

"For three thousand pounds."

"Yes, yes, I admit that I gave it up for three thousand pounds."

"So, you were not truthful with me."

"I may not have been as careful about what I told you as I might have been. What matters is that he could have allowed me a change of heart. It is that which most upsets me. It is why I so desperately wanted to exact my revenge with the stupid Georgi—"

He stopped his walking and turned to Elizabeth.

"You must forgive me. I am always aggravated by that man and especially how I now know he deceived you in describing things that happened in Ramsgate."

"I understand, Mr. Wickham. Mr. Darcy can bring out the emotional in even the most conservative of us. Now let us speak no more of it. I am satisfied."

They fell into a more leisurely stroll. After a minute, he said, "Might there then be a chance now that your mourning is concluded as has mine for us to...to be *something* to each other." His voice was low, although there was no danger of being overheard. Elizabeth was uncertain concerning what exactly he meant. She knew what she should say to this but found that she could not say it. To end all prospects with him. So she said nothing beyond that it was well past time for her to return to the Pratts' for the evening, notably not extending an invitation to him.

* * * *

ELIZABETH WAS AGAIN UP early the next morning. She dined with Pratt before he headed with Denny to the encampment. And she ventured out as she often did before Kitty was up. She carried a small note she'd written soon after returning from her rendezvous with Wickham. It read:

Mr. Darcy,

I hope you have not already left Brighton. If not and you have any inclination to speak further with me about what we spoke of recently, I should be happy to have you wait on me on the boardwalk to the west of the pier. If it is sunny, I will likely be shielding myself with a parasol, but I have every confidence that you will have no difficulty in identifying me.

I remain, &c., &c.,
Mrs. William Collins

At the Sussex Arms, she was told that the gentleman was still in residence. The note would be promptly sent to his room.

"He has already had his breakfast in the dining parlour," the man at the desk told her as he summoned a footman to bring the message up.

With a nod, Elizabeth left. She did not wish to encounter any familiar faces as she headed to the boardwalk, so she took something of a roundabout route to the west of the more travelled streets. Within ten minutes, she'd arrived. The boardwalk was filling with visitors wandering this way or that, often stopping at the railing to look out to the Channel and to those who'd ventured into it.

Not too far from the pier she saw an empty bench. There she sat, her parasol held awkwardly to block the sun. She expected, or at least hoped, that her wait would not be a long one.

This proved to be the case. Within only a few minutes, a somewhat out of breath Fitzwilliam Darcy approached her.

"Mrs. Collins. It was quite a pleasure to receive your note and as you can see, I was most excited about seeing you again."

She stood and they exchanged greetings.

"Shall we walk?" he asked and with a nod they began heading to the west, with Elizabeth mindlessly twisting her parasol back and forth over her right shoulder.

"I met with Mr. Wickham yesterday."

"And?" He did not appear surprised.

"I felt it incumbent upon me to afford him the opportunity to admit or deny the accusations that you have leveled against him."

"He denied them, of course."

"He did. Mostly, though, he claimed that you misunderstood his conduct."

"There was no misunderstanding, Mrs. Collins."

"I confess that I felt bound to refer to your sister given how significant that is to his history but there was very much I doubted in the defense he made to his misconduct."

She stopped and turned to him.

"I do not know if it matters."

He was struck by this unexpected utterance.

"How could it not matter?"

"Because, Mr. Darcy, I am not such a fool as he, and perhaps you, think I am."

"I don't—"

"Please Mr. Darcy. You insisted that I allow you to speak. Now it is my turn to insist that you do the same."

They resumed their walk in the bright sun.

"I was unsure when I left him and I cannot say I will not be tempted as to his charms in the future, much as I hope not to be. But he is far too dishonest and loose in his manner for me to respect him. And I confess to you, sir, that beyond all else I must respect a man if I have any hope of loving him."

She again stopped.

"There. I have said it. I believe I owe you these most intimate of my thoughts, sir, after the confidences you gave me in your and your sister's lives. That is all I wished you to know. And now, Mr. Darcy, you may return whence you came and not bother with another thought about me. I promise you that I am safe from Mr. George Wickham."

"Are you sure of this?"

"I tell you one more thing. The basis for my conclusion is not only what *you* have said of him. He had an innocent explanation for them. It is what his friends have said of him. I know they spoke the truth. They were proud of his debaucheries and gambling, I think. They perhaps envied it."

"Who do you mean?"

"Just some officers I've become acquainted with through my sisters and who served with him in the militia. His reputation as a womanizer and gambler is established and while it may have been exaggerated in some particulars as men—or at least *some* men—are wont to do regarding such things, I will not throw myself on one lacking in integrity. Say what you will of my dear Mr. Collins, he had much integrity and was an honest man."

She looked down and then back at him.

"That is what I say about George Wickham, and I beg of you, sir, not to have to speak of him again."

Darcy had never plumbed the depths of anyone's heart, perhaps not even his own, as this woman just did in her most remarkable way. There was nothing to be said to it and so all he did say was, "Well, thank you, Mrs. Collins. I am glad that I have been of service to you."

He bowed to her, and she curtseyed to him.

"I am afraid that I must return to London and then on to Pemberley in the morning. Pressing business. I will carry this conversation with me as I go and be grateful for the opportunity to have spoken and walked with you again."

"Thank you. When you see the Bingleys, please give him my warm regards and my sister my love."

"Yes, they are both still at Pemberley. It shall be done when I too arrive there, Mrs. Collins. Good day."

He turned but she interrupted his exit.

"Mr. Darcy, sir?"

He was again facing her.

"I am again greatly in your debt."

He bowed again.

"Thank you, ma'am," he said with a bow. And he was gone, again in the prompt manner that she'd become accustomed to seeing on the few occasions when they met.

* * * *

ALTHOUGH MR. WICKHAM shared dinner with the others that night, he did not stay long afterwards, complaining of a need to be home. When he was gone, Elizabeth told her sisters and in-laws that she'd decided to spend some time at Longbourn as she weighed what her future would be. What Kitty and Lydia believed this portended for her relationship with Mr. Wickham cannot be known but neither would be surprised if there was the happy news of a union by the month's end.

They were excited at that prospect but not at Elizabeth's going away after such a delightful stay (though the Pratts in particular were pleased for the return of their home to themselves and the...privacy that came with Elizabeth's departure, for neither of these Bennet girls had yet to become with child and each wanted the honour of being the first of the five Bennets to have that distinction).

Chapter 24. Mr. Wickham Speaks to Mr. Darcy

It was not long after the conference with Mr. Wickham that Elizabeth left Brighton to visit with her parents. She would be in Longbourn, though, only until Mr. and Mrs. Bingley settled in London, where a fine room would be ready for her in their house. And it was only a matter of a few weeks at Longbourn before Mrs. Collins was able to take up residence at No. 19, Mount Row.

Before she and her transportable belongings arrived in town, however, a slight (though significant) event occurred outside of *Darcy's* London house. As that gentleman himself neared the pavement on his way to his morning ride with Bingley, he was astonished to find himself face-to-face with George Wickham.

"I hope I am not disturbing you, Fitzwilliam."

Completely caught off guard by the unpleasant appearance, Darcy nearly fell back but recovered soon enough to respond, "The sight of you is always disturbing to me and other decent people."

"How you do not change. How you pretend that you and your few friends are the 'decent' ones."

"Wickham, it is not me but society that deems us so."

"Always the ass, Darcy. As I say, you do not change, and you never will."

"That may be the case, but I fear you have never changed since you were a spoiled, selfish child."

The two had stepped back onto the small area between the pavement and the house when the front door opened and Bradley, the butler, called, "Mr. Darcy. Are you alright? Is this gentleman bothering you?"

Darcy turned. "This man is no gentleman but no, Bradley, he doesn't bother me."

With a "very good, sir," Bradley went back inside only to appear a moment later at the window in the front sitting room.

"He's well trained, Darcy. Perhaps I should get myself one."

"With what? You have neither the money nor the temperament to keep a scullery maid let alone a proper butler."

"I assure you, sir, that I have more than enough money now."

"I understand how you got it, though I do confess to not understanding how you managed to keep it."

"That is was not given to me on a platter?"

"You are such an ungrateful—"

"Which does not matter. Much as I enjoy this line of talk, I came here on a more immediate task."

"Go on."

"You have poisoned my name with a worthy lady, and I will not have it. Were you half a man worth a duel I'd call you out. But I don't fancy swinging or wasting a shot or the blade of a sword on you. No, sir, I demand that you admit to Mrs. Collins that you don't know enough to condemn me to her."

"I surely do know enough."

"Arrogant as always. She told me of the accusations you made of me. Of how I tried to elope with Georgiana."

That Elizabeth had mentioned her revelation of this secret to Wickham at first angered him when she'd told him but he trusted her judgment that there was no alternative to doing so. He was quickly responding to Wickham: "You most assuredly did and would have gotten her and her money had I not fortunately appeared."

"As I told Mrs. Collins, there is no truth in what you say."

"No truth?" He laughed. "I was there, or do you not recollect that? She told me all."

"She was a girl with her illusions. I would never have taken her."

"Yet there you were, in Ramsgate with that...'governess' who deceived us so."

"Mrs. Younge? You are too stupid sometimes to be believed. Neither she nor I did anything wrong."

"I know what I saw. Fitzwilliam can vouch for it."

"Only he's in America and only all he knows is what you and perhaps Georgiana told him."

"She would not lie."

"She would not do anything to contradict her sainted brother. It was you she wanted to get away from with her fantasies of eloping, of becoming Mrs. George Wickham. Don't you see that?"

"I think I know her well enough to know her true feelings."

"You were like a father to her. I'll grant you that. She wouldn't confide anything to you. Oh, the things she told me about you."

"You are a liar."

"Darcy, it wasn't horrible things, I can assure you. Just that she sometimes felt like a caged bird and just wanted to fly. You never could see that. Nor could your cousin. Even now, you still can't."

"I will not withdraw what I said about you and my sister."

"Then, sir, I call you a scoundrel."

"As if anyone cares what you think."

"I believe Mrs. Collins does. Or at least did before you libeled me. With that and the business about the living your father promised me."

"Which you gave up for your thirty pieces of silver."

"Bastard...Yes, I did, but when I came crawling back to you, begging that you provide it to me after the law proved something of no interest to me, when there was no one else to take it, you still refused."

"You had your chance, and you gave it up, most willingly and, as I recall, squandered the money you got in a matter of weeks."

"That would not have mattered, Darcy, if you had acted with the consideration that I so loved in your father."

"Do not invoke the memory of my dear father. That is scandalous, sir. Scandalous."

"Still, sir. You have no defense to the wrongness of how you ultimately treated me in that respect."

Darcy did not deign to respond.

Wickham was not surprised by how the interview went. As he turned to leave, he said, "I will leave you to your bit of city riding. I regret that you have not been more reasonable, that you don't have the integrity and manners of acknowledging that you are not so certain of events as you were when you spoke of them to Mrs. Collins."

"I will not have you impugn my honour."

"It is not I who impugn it. It is you. By your actions. I say good day and wish you a pleasant ride."

With that and a very deep, very formal bow, George Wickham stormed away, trying to calculate how he might speak again with Mrs. Collins now that his desperate attempt to have Darcy speak on his behalf, or at least to withdraw his chief indictment, had failed.

Darcy watched him go. He was more anxious than he would have imagined possible in the confrontation. But he was late for his rendezvous with Bingley and could not afford to ponder on the matter any further.

Chapter 25. Elizabeth Consults with "Mrs. Bingley"

Elizabeth knew nothing of the Darcy-Wickham encounter when, less than a week after it took place, she moved into the Bingleys' grand house in Mayfair, not four blocks from Darcy's mansion. Caroline Bingley had ceded household responsibilities to Jane and moved in with her sister Louisa Hurst on Grosvenor Square. This was a relief to *all* concerned, and it did not take long for the two Bennets to fall into the comfortable pattern they'd long shared, enhanced, frankly, by the happiness that was washed over the elder and was pleasantly felt by the younger.

Elizabeth had emerged from her year of mourning the loss of her husband. With the help of Jane and of Charles Bingley, she entered that part of London society that the Bingleys inhabited, as well as the somewhat more prestigious one with which Darcy sometimes engaged.

Before her marriage, Elizabeth had adored country dances and assemblies, and within a month of her arrival in London, she and the Bingleys, often accompanied by Darcy and wearing dresses Jane insisted be made for her (on the Bingley account), attended dances and parties and balls and went to the theatre or opera.

"Will you confess something to me?" Jane asked one night when they'd not gone out but simply had dinner and enjoyed cardplaying with Darcy. The two were up in Jane's extremely fine and (at her husband's insistence) lavish French-style bedchamber. Jane sat on the small bench that faced the mirror on her dressing table, and Elizabeth made herself very much at home on the edge of the bed when the question was asked. She looked at her sister.

"What are your feelings for poor Mr. Darcy?"

"Mr. Darcy? Poor?"

"You know what I mean."

"Sadly, I do."

She looked down and then back. With a breath and recalling that never-sent letter to Jane she wrote at the Parsonage a lifetime earlier, she said, "Yes, I will confess that I have feelings for him. It's just that I am not sure what they are."

"What do you doubt?"

"He has so much. Handsome. Intelligent."

"Rich," Jane interjected.

"Yes, rich. I do enjoy my time with him. Very much. In some respects, I strangely enjoyed the time with him even when we first met, and I could barely tolerate him."

"And he you, as I recall."

"Yes, I do remember sharing that overheard view with you." She reached across to take Jane's extended hand. "But now it, well, is *different*. More pleasant. But I cannot, frankly, say in what capacity. Surely as a worthy opponent in many things."

"Oh, Lizzy. Do you have feelings for the *man*?"

"That's where my thoughts come undone. I *do* have feelings for him. Of that, I am sure. It is my not knowing the precise nature of those feelings that makes me so anxious. I have them, I can confess to you. I believe I have had them for some time, even if I didn't or couldn't admit it. But I do not know what they are."

Jane had turned herself on her little bench and was giving her full attention to her sister.

"Is there another? Do you hope you'll develop feelings for one we meet at a dance."

"There is no other, I promise you. Still, there are so many handsome suitors I see, even for a widow, and I don't know if should abandon them all. And…"

"And what?"

Elizabeth dropped her head to her hands and then lifted it again.

"I know I shouldn't but there is something about George Wickham that…attracts me to him."

"George Wickham!" Jane was shaken at this sudden and unexpected disclosure about a man who Elizabeth had told most of what she'd learned of him recently (*not* including the tawdry business in Ramsgate). "Did we not agree that he was a poor libertine who could not be trusted? Even if he is not so impoverished as he once was?"

"That's why I didn't want to mention him. I think...*know* he is that. But, Jane, I cannot be sure. Darcy is...Darcy. George Wickham is so much more entertaining. I like being with Darcy but there were times when I perhaps even loved being with Wickham."

"My God, you haven't...?"

"No. Of course not. Nor has he sought that from me. I think he is clever enough to know that to do so would terminate any future dealings with him."

"Yet you've been told by Denny and Pratt that he has done that, and probably worse, with other women," Jane said, increasingly anxious about what she was being told.

"I know, I know. But I feel he's different with me. When he was at Meryton, even Denny and Pratt admit that he displayed none of the debauchery he has at other times."

"I do not believe you are saying this. Charles told me how he confronted Darcy not long ago."

Now it was Elizabeth's turn to be surprised.

"What? You never told me. When?"

"It was only recently. He said Darcy told him that Wickham simply appeared at the house on Brook Street and, well, and demanded that Darcy admit to you that he was not so sure about what he said about Wickham."

"Wickham did have some defenses for Darcy's accusations."

"That must have been why he thought he could get Darcy to speak to you. And can it not be true that they are both respectable but simply each misunderstands the other?"

"Oh, Jane. Were I to have your confidence in the essential goodness of people. I am afraid in this, one of them must be wrong and one of them must be evil, at least in part."

"But in any case, why does it matter? You're not thinking of resuming a connection to Wickham."

"That's just it. I do not know. There are aspects of him that I do find...exciting and enchanting."

"Now you're sounding like a schoolgirl. Like Kitty or Lydia."

"Sometimes I wish I had their silliness for they will always be happy in their choices."

"Yes, but you are not them. You will never be happy unless in this instance you have chosen wisely."

"As I did not the first time I married?"

"Please, Lizzy. You must stop saying or even thinking that. As I've told you, we all know why you did what you did. Now, thank God—"

"And thanks to you marrying well."

"And marrying quite happily. Yes, who I married, I assure you, is no burden to me as who you married was to you. It does, however, free you to do what we always wanted to do. Marry for love. And do you love Wickham? Could you *love* Wickham even if what Darcy says about him is not true?"

"I don't know. You are right, though. I do think the qualities that I find so attractive in him are just the qualities that a scoundrel would have, and very much doubt if I can trust a man like that."

"I promise you; you could never be happy with a man you do not trust or respect."

Elizabeth flopped down on Jane's bed and waited until Jane was sitting on its edge and looking down at her in the way one or the other so often did at Longbourn when they were talking about what would make them happy as they grew old.

"I could never trust Wickham as I know you trust Bingley."

"And what about Darcy?"

"I think I could trust him. But I do not know if I could *love* him. And, of course, there remains the matter of his cousin who you've yet to meet."

"Miss Anne de Bourgh? Indeed, Not having met her is hardly one of the great burdens of my existence."

"My God. For you to say such a thing about someone! I have met her, and I assure you your not having done so is no burden to you. Darcy, though, remains in some form of commitment to her, and I am in fact surprised that they've not yet wed."

"I am not so unobservant to understand that you have something to do with his delay and hesitancy."

"Me? What could you possibly mean?"

"Now it is you who are being obtuse, and you know it. Don't tease me."

"I am sorry. He does have a strange tendency to want to come to my particular aid when he sees me in danger of making some catastrophic mistake. Do you not think it is because he is the great friend of my sister's husband?"

Elizabeth was on her side, her head cradled in her hand as she studied her sister.

"I will only tell you," said Jane, "that I have observed him to be particularly anxious when he is with us and you are expected but have not yet arrived and when you do come any liveliness of conversation from him ceases, or is at least suspended, until you are safely among us. He's also been known to steal a glance at you when you appear unobservant of him."

"Oh, I can assure you that I have noticed *that*, but it is something I have often noticed that men seem to do without themselves even realising it."

It had grown quite late, and Elizabeth finally was able to lift herself up from the comfortable spot she'd created for herself on Jane's bed. She told Jane that they both needed to retire and with a sisterly hug, she went to her room to contemplate what she and her dearest sister had just spoken about.

A day or two later, she visited her Aunt Gardiner. Though she was a familiar sight there, on this trip she had a particular purpose, and it was some weeks later that the purpose was finally realised. It was when her aunt appeared early one afternoon at the Bingleys' and sat with her niece in the corner of the house's fine sitting room.

There she handed Elizabeth the letter she received from Lambton, the town so near Pemberley. The letter, which hardly mattered anymore given Elizabeth's determination to have nothing further to do with George Wickham, nevertheless came as something of a shock, detailing salacious news—perhaps it was only gossip but there was a great deal of it—and involved several inappropriate connections between George Wickham and various women, young and old, in the neighbourhood (including, it was reported, the widowed Mrs. Younge).

Elizabeth felt guilty and dirty reading about the man. But not a shred of regret for having at long last removed herself—and she prayed it was for the final time—from him and his undeniable but she thought avoidable charms.

This determination was strengthened by several gentlemen Elizabeth met at events in town. More than anything, it was the meeting of one Michael Estridge. Estridge was still young, just five-and-twenty, and had been to Cambridge. He was the eldest son of a family of long-standing wealth and prestige in the County of Sussex, where there was a sizeable estate to which he was the heir (though his father was himself young and healthy Estridge himself told her early on and good naturedly). He effectively had his own house in town, and it was the home too of one of his sisters. Not the eldest, who was married, but the next, who was precisely Elizabeth's age.

Elizabeth was introduced to Estridge at a small ball being put on at a small house in Russell Square, and she enjoyed two dances with him and afterward sat at one end of a long table resting and getting refreshments and admiring the look of the man.

And he was a fine man to look at. He was tall and slim with hair in something of a libertine's fashion. Indeed, much of him could be characterised as being libertine and disarming. To Elizabeth, though, his eyes spoke of sincerity. If he was a rake, she wondered, was he the sort who could be reined in by a strong woman, as was not unknown to happen in some of her novels? For his eyes conceded a depth she'd never encountered with George Wickham, which set her to the realisation that at least on first impressions, Estridge's only *possible* equivalent was Fitzwilliam Darcy.

When Mr. Estridge paid a visit to the Bingleys the next day but one, her admiration of the man increased. When he was gone, Jane had to agree that there was "something about Mr. Estridge" that was quite appealing.

Whatever it was was enhanced when two days later both Jane and Elizabeth called on Mr. Estridge at his house in Bloomsbury so they could meet his aforementioned sister.

Miss Margaret Estridge was, as has been noted, nearly precisely Elizabeth's age and was also in search of a husband, though she had the luxury of being selective and the necessity of being cautious in that task thanks to the generous amount her father had set aside as her marriage settlement.

Margaret was a plain girl with straight black hair she generally kept in a cap. She had small eyes of an indeterminant colour nicely placed above a slight nose. Both Bennets took to her immediately and they promised to go out together in the coming days while Mr. Estridge sat awkwardly with his tea and biscuits, saying little until it was time for the visitors to leave.

It soon became a great pleasure for Elizabeth to walk with Margaret. Each took to visiting the other several days a week and with Jane learning the business of maintaining her new family's city house from Caroline—who'd slowly warmed to her sister-in-law Bennet if not the other one—it was often just the two. Having tired of taking turns around the various parks and greens in the neighbourhood, they often visited the small variety of nearby shops.

One held particular attraction to them both. James Johnson had established a bookshop on Bond Street some ten or fifteen years before. He was a burly man whose beard was white, though he himself was scarcely fifty. He maintained his shop with the joviality of a country auctioneer.

Soon Mrs. Collins and Miss Estridge were regular visitors to the establishment. Mr. Johnson would set upon them and other regular visitors the moment they were through the door. He kept a small stack of books for them and for other of his more genteel customers and would thrust one or two at them with an explanation of the plot and the author and the reason they would each enjoy reading it. For a select few of his lady patrons, he procured copies of an early edition of *Belinda*. Elizabeth and Margaret were among those allowed to share a copy of that version of Miss Edgeworth's book.

"My brother sometimes teases me about the books, and especially the novels I buy," Margaret said once when the pair was browsing one of the shop's narrow aisles, pulling the occasional volume out and asking Mr. Johnson whether she was likely to enjoy it. "At least he is not like my father, who had long been happy enough having me read some gothic fantasy tale and thinks my female mind not quite up to philosophy and history yet fears I'll get subversive or revolutionary ideas from things."

Margaret explained that her brother was quite unlike her father in his view of a woman's place. But, she said, father and brother did share a certain exasperation that although she'd come out years before she still had not entered into an engagement with someone eligible. She was, after all, in all relevant respects a quite attractive prospect.

She assured Elizabeth that she had no doubts that in time she would discover the proper man and he her. Just not as yet.

Chapter 26. Miss Estridge and Mr. Darcy

Although neither spoke to the other about it, both Margaret and Elizabeth considered whether Darcy would be the gentleman for Miss Estridge. Elizabeth had come to respect and admire her. She seemed much the superior of nearly everyone of Mrs. Collins's acquaintance. And given her growing regard for Darcy, she was determined to observe them both carefully to see whether there were glimmers of affection or perhaps more between the two.

Had she dared raise the subject with her friend, though, she would have saved herself the effort. For Margaret shared Elizabeth's view in many respects as to Fitzwilliam Darcy. He was a handsome man of fine breeding and quiet consideration. Indeed, in many ways he was as Elizabeth thought, that is, comparable in ways to Margaret's own brother.

And he also improved with familiarity, the familiarity of the quiet moments among friends, as sometimes happened when the Estridges and Darcy spent evenings together at the Bingleys'. For as Elizabeth discovered, and Margaret came to see, Darcy was very inadequate in the company of strangers but lively and kind with those who were his friends, a group that came to include both Estridges and, of course, Mrs. Collins.

So had Elizabeth asked Margaret whether she, Margaret, might have some attraction to Darcy, Margaret would have said something along the lines that she surely did and had Elizabeth asked whether she, Margaret, would consider exploring that feeling, Margaret would have said something along the lines that Fitzwilliam Darcy's heart had already been taken.

But Elizabeth had not asked the first of those questions and so she never reached the fact that was obvious to her friend that Darcy was in love with Elizabeth.

Which would have astonished Mrs. Collins. But not Darcy himself. For as Margaret had seen in her own quiet observation of the other two, Darcy's attentions were nearly exclusively on Elizabeth.

Darcy did not know but suspected that as a very clever but impoverished woman freshly out of mourning, Elizabeth would be interested in remarrying. He was aware, too, that the necessity of doing so was significantly eased by Jane's marriage to Bingley, but there was...too much woman in Elizabeth Bennet—as he still at times thought of her—to long delay her in falling in love.

Fitzwilliam Darcy had little to recommend himself to her and much—at least, he was certain, in *her* mind—against him. Yet more and more he was convinced that there was something of an omen in Mr. Collins's dramatic fall and death, however abhorrent and wrong he knew that thought to be.

His greatest concern was with the sudden appearance of Michael Estridge. As for George Wickham, he had no reason to believe he was attempting to renew his acquaintance with Elizabeth. Nor was anything heard further from Archibald Collins. But it was apparent that Mrs. Collins had become a great friend to Margaret Estridge. And it followed that the attentions to Miss Estridge must lead to attentions to Mr. Estridge.

It was in something like desperation, then, that he saw no alternative to acting. He was a cautious man. He took time to contemplate a situation. Once he decided what to do, though, he did it and he did it quickly.

And this was a situation he contemplated far more than any other in his life. He vividly recalled that conversation he had with his cousin Fitzwilliam in Sir Lewis's library at Rosings. Where he admitted, to himself as much as to his cousin, to ignoring his feelings for Elizabeth Bennet to his everlasting regret. About bemoaning to the Colonel having lost his chance to propose to Elizabeth Bennet or at least to advise her that such a proposal might be in the offing before she was betrothed to William Collins. Now, perhaps it was the low light or the heavy meal and sweet dessert or (most likely) the excellent claret, he could *see* that cousin, *with* him, sharing that wine in his musty old library.

Glass in hand, he paced the room. There was a leather chair he had turned to the room's centre. It was where Colonel Fitzwilliam sat.

"Darcy," *the imagined yet real officer called out,* "you will beat a hole in your fine carpet if you do not stop your pacing."

"I will stop when I know what I am to do."

"Darcy. You can be a horse's ass sometimes."

This imagined insult from this imagined person stopped him.

"What do you mean?"

"I mean, dear cousin, that you are pretending that there is a question when there is none. You are pretending that there is a doubt when there is none."

"I cannot be sure."

"Do you fear she will reject you? This simple country girl say 'no' to Fitzwilliam Darcy of Pemberley in Derbyshire?"

This had the desired effect. It made said Mr. Darcy angry.

"She is no simple girl, country or otherwise."

"You hardly know her."

"I know her well enough."

"Well enough for what?"

"To know that I wish to be with her for all of my days."

"And?"

"And that I fear I could not ever be happy knowing there is such a woman and that I failed for a second time to be honest with her and with myself about my feelings."

The imaginary cousin stood and placed his imaginary crystal glass of a first-rate claret on a side table.

"I have, you will recall, met this fine lady. She is no simple creature. Were she rich, you know, I might show an interest in her."

"And if you weren't in America."

"But I am in America so you are safe. From me."

"Though not from Mr. Michael Estridge."

"Cousin. I pray that I will be back in time for the wedding. If not, you must kiss the bride, your bride, for me."

With that he was gone, and Darcy was alone with his empty glass, and he stepped to the sideboard to refill it yet one more time.

Chapter 27. A Walk in the Rain

Morning emerged cold and wet. Darcy was up not long after the sun. He breakfasted early. The weather was too angry for a ride. He put on a slick coat and low hat and a pair of his most utilitarian boots and left the house even before nine. He could not stand waiting indoors.

The wind-driven rain slanted from west to east and was battering his face as he began his walk to Hyde Park, ignoring the puddles encountered on each street corner. It felt like a quite civilised stroll on a winter's day at Pemberley. He doubted that anyone else was braving the elements who did not have to.

He could not say for how long he walked, but the sun was high—in theory at least, the clouds still not having cleared themselves—and the rain had eased when he felt exhaustion pulling at him.

"Damn," he said aloud, though there was no one anywhere near to hear it.

It happened that his trek brought him out of the Park no great distance from Bingley's house on Mount Row. He was drenched, with water flooding over the rim of his hat and a sheen of cold rain plastered across his face. He felt none of it. It was horribly inappropriate, he knew, but he found himself standing at Bingley's door and pulling the house's bell cord hard.

There was no prospect of a visitor at this time or in this weather and it took longer than usual for the butler, buttoning his jacket, to open the door.

"Mr. Darcy, sir. You look a right mess, sir, you do. Come in, come in."

The door was opened wide, and Darcy was in the foyer, now dripping on its black-and-white checkered floor. In a moment the butler had taken Darcy's hat and gone around to Darcy's back and placed his hands so he could remove the drenched coat from the gentleman.

"Let me help you with that, sir," and Darcy was soon out of it.

A footman hurried into the foyer, and the butler handed the hat and coat, both dripping copiously, to him for hanging.

"I will get Mr. Bingley for you, sir."

"Thompson, wait."

The butler stopped and turned, looking quite confused.

"It is Mrs. Collins I wish to see. I know it is well early and out of time, but if she is at home, can you beg of her a minute or two of her time for me?"

The butler paused.

"Mrs. Collins, sir?"

"Indeed, Thompson. Mrs. Collins."

The footman returned and the butler instructed him to arrange for Mr. Darcy to get comfortable in the front sitting room and to clean up the puddle in the foyer while he went to see if Mrs. Collins was in.

Mrs. Collins was in. She was not dressed. There was no prospect of going anywhere for some time, at least until the weather changed for the better—it could hardly change for the worse—and she was perhaps more surprised than the butler that Mr. Darcy wished an immediate interview with her.

Quite in shock, she gave instructions that the visitor be told that she would be happy to wait on him and that she would be down presently. She asked that Bridget, her maid, be sent to her. When alone, she looked in the small mirror that sat above her dressing table. She was hardly presentable but there was no time for her to make herself so. The suddenness of the visit convinced her that she could ill afford to keep him waiting.

She combed her hair and placed it into one of her better caps just as Bridget appeared. A recently-acquired green housedress was draped across the corner of an oriental dressing screen and she was helped to put it on. With a pair of stockings and house slippers, she took another look at herself and decided she was tolerably passable and was soon heading down to find out what exactly Fitzwilliam Darcy was doing calling on her at this hour in this weather.

Chapter 28. A The Question

"What is it, Mr. Darcy? Is something wrong? Has something happened? Your sister perhaps?"

"Please, Mrs. Collins. You must allow me to speak."

Elizabeth was a bundle of confusion at the sight of the damp, disheveled man standing before her, nearly unrecognizable in his despair. After the exchange of courtesies, she lowered herself half into a chair, not once moving her eyes from him.

For his part, his eyes looked everywhere but at her as he moved slightly to one side then the other. Finally, those eyes locked on hers. It frightened or at least startled her.

"Marry me."

His eyes broke from hers and he turned away violently.

"Marry you?"

He stepped to the window that was being rattled by the storm before thrusting himself back towards her, dropping to a knee and reaching, involuntarily, for her hand. She did not have the presence of mind—perhaps she was in want of the presence of control—to refuse it to him. His was wet but she barely noticed as a flood of emotions quickly ran through her.

"Yes, Mrs. Collins. Let me strip you of that name we know we both abhor and take mine for it. You will learn to like it, to be Mrs. Darcy, I hope in time. I promise you I will love it from the first moment I can speak it."

She pulled her hand away but still bent towards him.

"Mr. Darcy, you astonish me. What brings this strong and perhaps temporary fever on."

He was wounded. "I can assure you, Mrs. Collins, that it is no fever and even if it is, it will never break. I will withdraw quickly and never broach the subject again should that be your desire, however painful it will be to me. But I can wait no more. I love you and I wish to marry you. It is quite simple."

"I will not wonder at your feelings towards me. But I will need some convincing with respect to your *conduct* towards me and towards my family."

"Mrs. Collins, I have plainly confessed to having wronged your family and especially your dear sister. You know, however, that I have endeavoured, with some success you will admit, to having atoned for that misjudgment. You must acknowledge, ma'am, that that judgment was exercised with the best of intentions as to my dear friend and, as I said, that when I realised it was a mistake I remedied it, with your help."

"I acknowledge it and that you have always been truthful to me. Unlike some others."

This last was said nearly under her breath, but he heard it clearly.

"I assure you, Mr. Darcy," she continued, "that I have not for a moment questioned the constancy of your character or your honesty. You have been hurtful at times with that honesty as to me—"

"Mrs. Collins, I admit that my prejudice towards you and, I fear, at times towards your family and your situation may have inclined me in what I recognise were selfish and perhaps even childish ways. That my initial feelings for you were decidedly not what they currently are."

"What of your cousin?"

"Colonel Fitzwilliam?"

"No, Mr. Darcy. Anne de Bourgh?"

"Oh goodness. I confess to you now and we never need speak her name again, though I will tell you that I believe her at heart to be a good woman who is too sheltered and isolated by her mother. I dearly care for Lady Catherine, but I am not such a fool as not to see her as she is. But regarding Anne. Yes, I do understand that Lady Catherine fervently wishes that she and I marry."

"Mr. Darcy," Elizabeth interrupted, the man still on one knee before her, "you seem terribly uncomfortable. Please at least stand, sir, so I need not look down at you."

"Oh, Mrs. Collins, it is more me looking up to you, which I have come to do often."

"Mr. Darcy, you are losing your train of thought. Sit here," and she motioned to a chair beside her, "and your dampness will not do too much injury to it." He rose and, flinging the tails of his jacket to either side of himself, half-sat beside her, never turning from the object of his desperate attention. Had he not loved her before, he surely would have now, and he saw how fresh and vibrant that face was as it somehow smiled at him.

For Elizabeth's part, her initial shock had fluttered away, replaced by her own feelings. They reappeared in full force and grew a thousand-fold, a mixture of emotions, strange and strangely entirely natural to her. When he was settled, she reached her hands across and he took them gladly and expectantly.

When they were thus settled, he resumed.

"Anne is in the end, I think, a sweet creature and you will come to like her, I think, once this obstacle of her mother's expectations is removed."

"Will your aunt allow them to be removed?"

"I am in the perhaps enviable position of not being compelled to bow to the wishes of my aunt. Or anyone else for that matter. My confession to you, though—and it may be in some respects sinful—is that I fully intended to propose to Anne, as by that time seemed natural given that I had yet to come upon a woman to whom I could lose my heart. Excepting one."

"'Excepting one'?"

"You will not remember it, but not long before your husband died, I visited Rosings Park with my cousin, the Colonel. I was told by my aunt that her dreary clergyman and his arrogant wife were to share dinner with us the next evening."

Oh, how I remember that!, Elizabeth thought.

"I realised how often I drifted to thoughts of you even after you had accepted Mr. Collins's hand. Then the mere thought of seeing you, of being in the same room as you, had a disturbing effect on my equilibrium. My initial intent of proposing to Anne on that trip—for proposing to her was a major reason for the journey in the first instance—vanished until I could banish whatever had arisen in me about you.

"As I said, these were quite inappropriate feelings, if feelings they were. I could not leave soon enough."

"I do remember how you and the Colonel fled the next morning."

"I feared disturbing you and your husband as we rode back to London, but it could not be helped."

"So, you left in such a hurry because of me?"

"Precisely. I knew, though, that the unfinished business as to Anne needed to be resolved, so I sought and was granted an invitation from Lady Catherine to return. It was days before we were to do so that I received a letter from Anne advising me of the unfortunate accident that befell Mr. Collins.

"This news was delivered in a matter-of-fact manner, so that the Colonel and I would not be surprised by encountering a house in mourning when we came and asking that we delay the trip for several days so that the activities surrounding the death and the burial were concluded. We of course agreed."

Elizabeth thought of those difficult days and was reminded of the callous treatment she felt at the hands of both Lady Catherine and her daughter.

"This is where my confession is required. For I thought that Mr. Collins's death might be an...an omen concerning you."

"Me?"

"Yes. You. Was your being released from your marriage to Mr. Collins even in this horrible fashion a sign that I should pursue what I was increasingly coming to realise I *felt* for you? So, all thoughts of proposing to Anne de Bourgh were banished from me and I have been...confused as to whatever feelings I had and have as to you, though I have not acted on them beyond the very slight services I have endeavoured to perform for you."

Elizabeth found this disconcerting.

"Is that why you altered your attitude towards Jane?"

"It was not. I did what I did in that respect when I realised how I had wronged my friend, and your sister as well. That it gave me the opportunity to have frankly intimate conversations with you was an enhancement, but it was not my motivation. I had done wrong, and I was under the obligation to correct it. Recall that I had no inkling that you had any feelings for me."

He paused and gave her something of an intimate smile. "Indeed, Mrs. Collins, in this lengthy conversation you have yet to give any indication of that rather important fact."

"Oh, Mr. Darcy, I cannot believe you say that, for I always understood you to be an observant man. I have not *said* anything along those lines but surely you must have *seen* the increasing pleasure that I have in being in your company."

"I will confess this too, that your countenance in my presence has improved over our recent encounters but I didn't dare hope that they were an indication of anything beyond familiarity."

"I assure you, sir, that it is far more than familiarity. And I, too, must confess, and my confession is decidedly more sinful than anything you have done."

"I cannot imagine that."

"You need not imagine it. I confess it to you, and only to you, that at that time I did write of my, a married woman's, inappropriate thoughts of you to Jane, in a letter I promptly destroyed, never intending that it be sent."

Darcy was quite confused by this roundabout way of speaking.

"You see, I recall that trip that you and the Colonel took to Rosings quite well myself. My dear Mr. Collins told me that you were coming and that we were invited to dine with you. He was beyond excitement at the prospect. I was awash in quite distinct emotions for I had given you scant thought since, as you said, I accepted Mr. Collins.

"The thought of seeing you, of being in the same room as you the very next day were enough to set me into the greatest anxiety. And it was as I was trying to compose myself the next morning on my walk—"

"That you ran into me, who was endeavouring to do much the same thing."

"Indeed. I could barely speak or think or anything in that brief encounter."

"Which I ended so rudely and so abruptly."

"Now, Mr. Darcy, I begin to see why. I had no reason to think you were anything but...rude."

"Had I had my head about me, I may have done better but as I say I did not and was forced to retreat to collect myself. And then we were cordial enough at dinner."

Elizabeth stood, and Darcy immediately did as well.

"Mr. Darcy, I think we have delayed long enough. Ask me your question and I will give you my answer, with the assurance that I have used this delay to order my thoughts and emotions so that I am in a position to respond."

Darcy reached for her hands, and they were gladly extended. Had they noticed, each would have felt the sweat that had accumulated on the other's. But they did not notice anything but their looks and his words.

"Mrs. Elizabeth Collins. Will you do me the honour of becoming my wife?"

"Mr. Fitzwilliam Darcy. There is nothing I desire more than becoming your wife. And partner."

This addition did not surprise him, and he was pleased by it. Anne or any of a thousand other women could be his *wife*. The only woman in the world who could be his *partner* stood before him, her hands in his, and had just agreed to it. He leaned down slightly, and she pushed herself up slightly so their lips could meet, and they kissed.

Chapter 29. A Most Pleasant Interview

While Elizabeth was a widow and of age and did not require her father's consent to be married, Darcy insisted. The next day after their agreement, and the sharing of the fine news with the Bingleys themselves, the two lovers took a Darcy chaise to Longbourn. Their visit was not announced, and it took some minutes for Mr. and Mrs. Bennet to make themselves presentable to their visitors, who waited patiently in front of the house.

Mrs. Bennet was beyond shocked at the appearance of the man she'd long found barely tolerable, and then solely insofar as he was a great friend of her son-in-law. Now here he was alone with her Lizzy!

Mr. Bennet, too, was surprised and had the wit to immediately understand the meaning of the appearance. He'd long found Darcy a proud, unpleasant sort of man from the little he had seen of him and especially from what Elizabeth's mother and sisters had said of him. Still, he'd long had confidence of this particular daughter's good judgment—most painfully in her acceptance of Mr. Collins under all the circumstances—and it was difficult to square the two as they approached, particularly given the smile she'd rarely displayed in the time since she'd left as a new bride.

Darcy stopped before the two elder Bennets and gave a deep bow.

"Mr. Bennet. Mrs. Bennet. It is my great pleasure to see you both looking so well."

"And you, sir," Mr. Bennet was able to say, his wife being left in an unprecedented state of muteness as she came to realise why this horrible man was there.

"Mr. Bennet. I beg that I have a moment of your time."

After a quick glance at his Lizzy and a smile and nod from her, he said, "Mr. Darcy, it is my pleasure. Come join me in my library. We shan't be disturbed there."

When they were seated, with Elizabeth and her mother pretending to shield themselves in the house's shrubbery where they could see into the room, Mr. Darcy was direct in asking for Elizabeth's hand.

"And I assume that Mrs. Collins has agreed to give it to you," Mr. Bennet said, more formally than he intended.

"She has indeed, sir. She has condescended to make me the happiest of men."

This was enough for Mr. Bennet to question to himself whether this was the same Fitzwilliam Darcy that he'd met rarely and about whom he heard much.

"As to this daughter more than any other," he replied. "I defer to *her* judgment." He leaned forward. "I will tell you, sir, that she once married out of necessity, and I believe she regretted it more than she will ever admit. I will consent to your connection with her, but I make it conditional."

"Conditional?"

"I will interview her and if she convinces me that she wishes to marry you out of affection and love, I will be even more glad than I was about her sister Jane. I should not say it, but she has long been my favourite and I would not part with her again for anything less than true love and affection."

"Sir, I have no hesitancy in assuring you that *I* would not take her on if I did not believe that she and I shared true love and affection. I respect her far too much and I believe she respects me in the same manner."

He stood.

"We should not delay. I will ask her to come speak to you." He looked out the window and could see the two ladies anxiously awaiting the results of the gentlemen's interview. "While she is here," added Darcy. "I will endeavour to make myself more agreeable to your fine wife."

He gave a short bow and left to fetch his great love.

When she arrived in the library, her father was standing. He closed the door and directed her to one of the pair of chairs on which he and Darcy had sat. He remained standing and then began walking about the room, looking grave and anxious. "Lizzy," said he, "what are you doing? Are you out of your senses, to be accepting this man? Have not you always hated him?"

"Oh, papa," she said, "I have been a great fool twice in my life. You know the first, but I now realise the second, my great prejudice against Mr. Darcy. I promise you, it has grown and grown within me until I could no longer control it."

"What, my dear?"

"It was a quiet affection that I did not even understand until it had grown and grown into…love. I can say no more but that now it is love."

He dropped into the chair beside hers. He reached across for her hands and controlled their shaking.

"I confess that I've never known it in the way you mean. But I have well known it as to you." Elizabeth's tears were welling up and she pulled her right hand from him to stem the tide that was growing on her cheek and his fingers joined hers there.

He smiled. "I see that you are determined to have him. He is rich, to be sure, and you may have more fine clothes and fine carriages than Jane. But all I ask is whether he will make you happy? Any objections that I or anyone else may have—"

"Oh, papa, she of whom you speak will be sure to have quite the alteration in view once she learns of our interview and" (she nodded to the window, where they could both see Mrs. Bennet and Mr. Darcy standing awkwardly beside one another, not unlike a similar scene some time earlier when Mr. William Collins was the petitioner, and continued) "learns to enjoy his presence."

He laughed. "It would go more easily with her had he been in regimentals. No, Lizzy, I have every confidence in you, and we all know we owe you a great debt of gratitude and that you deserve all the happiness you can get. As you believe that Mr. Darcy will give you quite enough of that, and since I know that you could never be happy unless you truly esteemed your husband and it is plain in just these few minutes that you do, I will consent."

"Will?" she asked.

"Oh, Lizzy, I am not such a fool as to not make my initial consent to him conditional on our little interview. To his credit, Mr. Darcy had no doubt that you would do exactly as you have done. So, we must tell him that all of the conditions placed on my consent have been satisfied and that I will be thrilled and excited, so far as I can be thrilled and excited by anything—"

"Oh, papa."

"No, Lizzy, we must not suffer any illusions about my own deficiencies. I will be thrilled and excited about having him as a son-in-law. I truly will."

And with that, the two Bennets removed themselves from Mr. Bennet's library and were set upon quickly when they emerged from the house by Mrs. Bennet and Mr. Darcy and to the latter Mr. Bennet extended his hand and said, "Sir, I am overjoyed with the good fortune my Lizzy seems to have come upon. I said I would not settle on anything less than she deserves and she has convinced me that she is not settling by marrying you and I am overjoyed by the prospect."

Mrs. Bennet understood the gist of this oration and decided that having a rich if proud man as a son-in-law was tolerable given that Kitty and Lydia had gotten themselves fine officers. She crooked her arm so that Fitzwilliam Darcy could lead her into the house for some refreshments.

Chapter 30. Walking With Miss Estridge

"Just be glad it wasn't like in that novel," Margaret said as she and Elizabeth took their walk a few days later and well after the joyous (and not surprising to Miss Margaret Estridge) news was shared.

"Novel?"

"You have surely read it. The one where the eldest son was secretly engaged but fell in love with someone else."

"Yes, I know it. Where his mother cut him off when she learned of the engagement and when he had no money, the girl he was to marry rid herself of him and married his younger brother."

"Who got all the money. But *he* got the woman he really wanted."

"And enough money for them to live on, quite frugally as a clergyman, I think."

The two were just entering Hyde Park.

"Well, Lady Catherine does not control my Darcy's fortune so there was no danger of that happening."

"But she will be very cross."

"Oh, she will. As is your brother, I suppose."

"Oh, him. Yes. He might have made advances towards you in time."

"I did notice how his eyes sometimes lingered on me."

"I think men are quite naïve as to that and he often reddened when he caught me catching him doing it. I'm sure he would have pursued you were I not his sister and your friend and that such restraint would have been washed away in time. But between us you're better off without him, which is a sister's prerogative to say."

And as they ventured deeper into the park, they laughed about the close calls any number of people had before Darcy proposed to Elizabeth.

Chapter 31. A Most Unpleasant Interview

Confirmation of Lady Catherine's reaction to the news of her nephew's offer and the parson's widow's acceptance was not long in coming. Darcy felt bound to fly to Rosings on the morning after he and Elizabeth were back from Longbourn. He would deliver the news himself. An express was sent early in the morning to advise his aunt of his arrival "with news that I hope you will find pleasant." He very much doubted that sentiment, but he thought it worth suggesting.

She was only just up when he arrived on horseback at the great house. After getting himself presentable in a room off the kitchen, the butler directed him to his aunt's study. It was not as large as Sir Lewis's library was—that room, which was where Darcy and Colonel Fitzwilliam had their first conversation about Elizabeth, the woman who Darcy then believed he had forever lost, was largely untouched since the man's death—but had a nice aspect off to the northeast. The wall coverings were light and pleasant (and quite expensive) and the furniture of chairs and tables and a desk were light in colour (and quite expensive) as well.

When Darcy was announced, Lady Catherine was alone except for Anne and Mrs. Jenkinson, and only those two stood at Darcy's entrance. He bowed to Anne and her minder, and they curtseyed to him, somewhat tentatively. Lady Catherine herself sat on a very fine French settee, leaning against one arm with a French tea set on a table beside it.

"Darcy. What could it be for you to come rushing here so quickly with only an express this very morning to tell me you would be here? Is it, nephew, to do with Anne?"

Anne looked from her mother to her cousin when this was said. "You say," and Lady Catherine lifted the paper and placed her spectacles on to read and leaned close to it, "'I hope you will find it,' the news, 'pleasant.'" She placed it down on her lap. "What ever can you mean? It concerns Anne, does it not?"

Again, her daughter looked at her and then down at her hands, tightly bunched in her lap.

"Lady Catherine. It does not concern my dear cousin directly. I will not stray from my objective. I came here to tell you the joyous news that I have offered my hand and my fortune to Mrs. Elizabeth Collins."

Lady Catherine's head shot up almost as quickly as did Anne's.

"Mrs. Collins? The widow of my dear parson? You surely do not mean *her*."

"I most surely do mean her, aunt. I love her ardently."

"Love? Surely you have no notion of that. And even if you do, nephew, you must resist those…urges and understand your duty. Your duty, sir."

"My duty now is to her."

"Preposterous. Your duty is to me. *To your family*. Your mother and I agreed that you would marry Anne and marry Anne you shall. We have been waiting" (and at this she thrust her arm in her daughter's direction and Anne seemed to sink into her chair as if she had nothing to do what was being said) "to finally do what we *all* know must be done. It is your duty!"

Darcy was standing throughout this and had moved not an inch. His aunt rose, letting Darcy's express paper fall to the ground. Anne rushed over to help her.

"I don't need you, child," she said with anger or sympathy or some other emotion to her offspring. Anne backed away, and turned to look at her cousin, and he somehow seemed taller than he ever had. He was very much taller than his aunt.

"You will not do it. I forbid it! It shall not be done. The idea of that woman, who is of no respectability and was barely civil on those occasions when I offered the hospitality of the de Bourgh family to her without conditions. Who has no accomplishments of any value so far as I can tell. Who was blessed, I say, to get Mr. Collins, rest his soul, and can aspire to go no higher than she was with him. If I were to give any thought—which I assure you I have not—it was that she is far better off remaining a clergyman's widow for the rest of her dreary days."

"You do not know her," Darcy said flatly.

"And you do? I know her well enough and you, sir, are a fool. Men are too often fools. Only my sweet Lewis and perhaps your dear father had an ounce of sense about them. I tell you, Fitzwilliam, that I thought you too were graced with that. From my sister's blood and your father's."

She sat back down heavily.

"It shall not be. You believe yourself to be free to do as you please. You think you are free to make a fool of yourself with that girl. But you are not free to besmirch your family, *our* family, and its name and its reputation. To pollute Pemberley, for that is what bringing that girl would amount to. You would be a laughingstock among all the decent families."

Darcy remained stoic to this onslaught.

"And don't think you will be welcome here. You will not be, nephew. You will have cut off me and my daughter and everything that we hold dear and that you, too, should hold dear." She bent to the floor from the settee, reaching for the express. When she clutched it, she lifted it. She waved it at her nephew. "'I hope you will find it pleasant,'" she recited from memory.

"Far from it," she said as she flung the innocent paper in his general direction, and it fell to the floor well short of the mark.

"I am greatly displeased. You may go now. You have come on a fool's errand, and I shall not be subjugated to you a moment longer." She reached behind her to pull the cord and the door opened. Neither Anne nor Darcy moved for a moment.

He turned to his cousin. He bowed. "Anne, I do regret if my decision has displeased you. I hope you in time will understand that if what I do is unpleasant to you, I am greatly sorry." He bowed again.

He turned back to his aunt. "I am sorry, aunt. I understand you are disappointed and I daresay that my mother too would be disappointed. I have thought much on the decision I have made. It is the correct one. I do not regret having made it. My only regret is that it will adversely affect my future dealings with you and with my dear cousin. I fear, Lady Catherine, that that cannot be helped, and I must beg your forgiveness for that."

With a final bow, he turned towards the door and was gone. Had his aunt deigned to go to a window at the front of the house she would have seen him quickly leaving Rosings Park to return to London.

For her part, his cousin did leave her mother and did go to a room at the front of the house and did see her cousin race away on his horse. And she admitted to herself that she found the news he brought to have been quite pleasant indeed.

Chapter 32. The News from Brighton

Kitty and Lydia were through the door at the Bingleys' so quickly that Thompson was nearly knocked to the ground. They each called up from the foyer, "Jane, Lizzy, we are here. We have such news."

They tossed their bonnets and travel coats to the footman who'd joined the butler and the pair of Bennet girls were soon ascending the broad staircase calling to their slothful sisters, it being nearly noon and they not being down to greet them.

That Elizabeth had already been out for over an hour walking with Margaret Estridge did not signify to Kitty and Lydia. Neither she nor Jane was down when they arrived and that was just too, too much for them!

Elizabeth quickly emerged from her room in a morning gown and Jane soon joined her as they looked down to the first-floor landing.

"You must come down, Jane and Lizzy, we have such horrible gossip to add to Lizzy's news of agreeing to marry that Mr. Darcy," Lydia said before she and Kitty raced down whence they came and into the sitting room to await their elder—they something laughing referred to them as their "elderly"—sisters.

When Jane and Elizabeth managed to get their decrepit bodies into the sitting room, where refreshments had been arranged and Kitty and Lydia had had the opportunity to freshen up after their hurried journey to London from Brighton, the sisters sat in a cluster of chairs near the front window.

"First, of course, we came to congratulate you, Lizzy," Lydia said, and Kitty quickly echoed this.

When Elizabeth had appropriately acknowledged their happy wishes, Lydia quickly said, "but you cannot imagine what has become of your George Wickham."

In fact, perhaps the last person Elizabeth wished to hear news about was that man, who she'd well and largely forgotten.

"Yes, Lizzy," Kitty said, "he has for some weeks been seen promenading with an older woman—"

"It turns out to be a widow he *knew*" (and Lydia laughed at that word, which she spoke slowly and deeply) "from when he was a youth—"

"It was a Mrs. Young or something. Though she surely ain't that!"

"Yes, Mrs. Younge, with an 'e,'" Lydia clarified. "It was a Mrs. Younge who was from around that house of Darcy's and who was, we are informed, the governess of that sister of Darcy's."

"Georgiana," Elizabeth said.

"That's the one. He only has the one, much younger sister, right?" Lydia asked.

"Indeed, and he is her guardian," Elizabeth added.

"Well, the whole town was gossiping about her. The woman Wickham's been favouring. She's old and ugly and doesn't have sixpence to her name—"

"And then two weeks ago they read the first banns!"

Elizabeth was stunned. It didn't matter to her, but being familiar with George Wickham, she found this information of interest, particularly as it concerned Mrs. Younge, about whom Elizabeth knew more than she cared to. She wondered what Darcy and especially Georgiana would feel at this news, but her thoughts were quickly interrupted by Lydia.

"Denny, of course, invited the two to visit when they were in Brighton, and they came. She was with him and, as I say, she was old and ugly and shriveled up, but he does seem to have a fondness for her, though I cannot see it."

"My Pratt and I were there too, and he seems happy enough with his choice. He don't need the money as he's kept to his vow about not gambling, since he'd lose everything if he did, and I think she'll keep him from it—"

"And from some of the ladies in the neighbourhood—"

"Yes, Lizzy, from some of those ladies."

And the two younger sisters laughed at George Wickham, and Jane and Elizabeth genuinely hoped that this Mrs. Younge was a good influence on him and his wayward conduct and they were happy for him (and for some of those "ladies").

Chapter 33. A Secret Note

Late on the afternoon of the day after Darcy returned to London from his interview with his aunt, an express arrived at the Bingleys'. It was addressed to "Mrs. Collins/Confidential." When Elizabeth was alone in her room, Bridget knocked on her door. She had a silver tray on which the letter was placed. The addressee took it and waited until the maid was gone to open it. She recognised the seal; it was Anne de Bourgh's, seen long before in her final days at the Parsonage.

Dear Mrs. Collins,

I have come to understand that I was not as considerate to you while you resided in Hunsford as I should have been. I hope in time you will forgive me.

I write on an extremely confidential basis regarding your forthcoming marriage to my cousin. I assure you that I am pleased for the both of you. I have known Fitzwilliam for nearly my entire life and he has been a bit of light in what has come in recent years to be my somber world. Of all people, you are the one who can appreciate his ability to bring joy into a person's being. He has done that for me in a most brotherly way, though I pray you never disclose this to him, in his visits to Rosings and in my too infrequent journeys to Pemberley or even to town to see him.

I have long known my mother's intentions as to him with regard to myself. I will admit that part of me hoped that those intentions would come to fruition. You again will understand this part of me. I harboured such hopes until the moment he told my mother and me that he had selected you as his bride and that you had accepted. Witnessing his enthusiasm and having some experience with you impressed upon me that you are the only woman who can make him happy.

This is a difficult confession to make, to cede my own inadequacies in this regard. Fear not, though. For I understand that it is far better that I have a contented cousin than one who married me solely from obligation and without <u>husbandly</u> affection. And it is far better, too, that I have him as a friend and that you too may come to have filial feelings towards me.

I believe that this is the reason for my writing. I cannot say when we will cross paths again. I pray that when we do, you look to me as a companion and not as a rival for that good man's affections, for knowing him I am assured that he has given all of those manly affections to you.

I realise that this letter is not diplomatic in some respects. I beg that you destroy it but hold close to yourself the sentiments I am so very pleased to express herein.

I ask that you keep my thoughts close save in one particular. I ask that you, in confidence, disclose my sentiments and express my fondest wishes to my dearest of cousins, who I fully expect will soon become the dearest of husbands.

> With fondest wishes,
> Your soon-to-be cousin
> (Miss) Anne de Bourgh

Chapter 34. Miss Georgiana Darcy

It was readily agreed that the wedding would take place in the church in Meryton, the one where Jane married Bingley. And Jane would stand with her sister as Bingley would stand with his friend. They would travel to Derbyshire, with the Bingleys, after the ceremony.

But not before Elizabeth met one additional person. That was Georgiana Darcy. Elizabeth knew much about her from others, stretching from Wickham all the way to Jane, who'd met the girl—near a woman now—during her stay at Pemberley. Georgiana had been at the estate most of the time since the Ramsgate fiasco with Mr. Wickham and Mrs. Younge, except for a brief period when she was in London. That was when Mr. Collins was still alive.

Georgina did not much like town. She'd come out, of course, but her shyness and great wealth made her seem distant, and she was happy when her brother sent her to the country. When news that he was getting married reached her in a pair of letters, she hurried south so that she could attend and was settled into the house on Brook Street well over a week before the ceremony.

Two letters?

There was her brother's. It was much as things tended to be between them—Wickham spoke the truth when he described the relationship between the Darcys as almost paternal—that is, direct and to the point.

The second was from Elizabeth herself.

Miss Georgiana Darcy
Pemberley, Derbyshire

My Soon-to-Be Sister,

I instructed your brother to indicate that his letter to you must be opened before this one and I presume that you have followed this most natural of protocols. Having done so, you will know that your brother has offered me his hand in matrimony and I have taken it. And he will take my hand and all the rest of me too!

I cannot say what you know of me from either <u>your</u> brother or <u>my</u> sister but I assure you that their words are far, far more flattering than I—or I daresay anyone who is spoken of by a future beloved partner or longtime beloved sister—could possibly be and I hope that you will find me at least adequately pleasant when we are finally introduced to one another.

This is all I will say to you now. I insisted that I write to assure you of my enthusiasm about becoming a Darcy and becoming your sister. Please hurry to town as quickly as you may be carried so I can meet the woman about whom I have heard so many fine things.

> *Your (soon-to-be) Sister*
> *Elizabeth*

The point will not be belaboured here that both Darcy and Jane had extoled Elizabeth's value and that when she did arrive in London not five days after receiving the two letters, Georgiana found Elizabeth far closer to what the others said of her than what Elizabeth said of herself.

What became of that, however, is for another telling. For now, it is enough that all the participants in the wedding have been introduced. It was held barely a month after the two agreed to be one another's forever—subject as they were both well aware to the vicissitudes of life and death—Elizabeth stood with Mrs. Bingley and Darcy stood with Mr. Bingley and they exchanged vows and so much more with each other in the Meryton church.

Much as was the case when Jane was married, the church was full of well-wishers from Longbourn and Meryton, and they were joined by Mr. and Mrs. Bennet, Georgiana, all of the Bennet girls and their husbands, Mr. and Mrs. Sebel and Charlotte's parents and siblings, the Philipses and the Gardiners, Caroline Bingley and Mr. and Mrs. Hurst, Margaret Estridge and her brother Michael, and Mr. Archibald Collins.

While neither of the de Bourghs appeared, that was hardly a burden to those who did. It was widely regretted, though, that Colonel Fitzwilliam was still deep into his regiment's engagement somewhere in America—the United States as they insisted on calling themselves—and it would be some time before his congratulatory message could reach his great friend and the woman the Colonel long suspected was destined to become Mrs. Darcy.

As to those who could and did attend, Archibald Collins had concluded (or at least was able to convince himself) some time before that Jane would not have suited him at all and he was quite content to live the life of a young, bachelor lawyer with a fine house in town with his meals at his club and a housekeeper coming in thrice a week.

It was the case that two of the shyest among the guests managed to arrange to meet when they were both back in London so that Margaret Estridge took great joys out of acting as something of a guide to the places and ways of town for Georgina Darcy. While her brother and new sister were away in the north, she began to feel an attachment to Michael Estridge, Georgiana did, and it was many the day when the three of them could be seen in the upper reaches of Hyde Park.

It was also the case, much to Mrs. Darcy's disbelief, that Caroline Bingley seemed to have accepted that she was not the woman for Darcy after all and turned out to be something of an older sister, at least in Elizabeth's absence, to Georgiana. And in her quieter moments, Mrs. Darcy admitted to herself that she may have erred in her initial judgment of that woman as she had with respect to several men.

And whether Caroline Bingley found something approaching immediate attraction with the prospect of eventual affection is, sadly, also for another telling.

Chapter 35. Pemberley

It was a wonderfully clear day, sparkling but not warm with only a few fluttering clouds drifting about as the Bingleys and the Darcys passed through Lambton *en route* to Pemberley. With each mile, Elizabeth Darcy—Elizabeth Collins as was, (Elizabeth Bennet before that)—felt increasingly anxious to finally see her new country home and the estate of which she was now mistress.

Their landau approached from the south with the top down. The two men sat facing the rear in order that their wives might have the benefit of the view before them. As they approached Pemberley Woods, Elizabeth's excitement could hardly be contained as Jane gripped her hand. She knew that her new life would truly begin when she crossed into the small forest. The park was very large, and it took some time to cover it. The others remained quiet to allow the bride to explore for herself what in recent weeks she'd begun to imagine.

They entered the Woods at a low point. After some minutes, the carriage emerged into the daylight. Across the valley she caught sight of Pemberley House, which was reached after some descending, a bridge crossing, and a rising. The great house was in and out of view as they approached it until it appeared, like a sort of Biblical vision, rising majestically as the four fine horses and the carriage with its occupants climbed the final incline. They soon reached its front.

Lined up as pretty as one could wish was the staff, the entirety of the servants in the house and all those who tended to the grounds and to the horses. As the landau stopped, Williams, the butler, rushed to open its door.

"Welcome to Pemberley, Mrs. Darcy," he said with a deep bow and a northerner's accent. She took his offered hand, and she stepped down to the gravel and Mrs. Bingley was soon beside her, closely followed by their husbands.

Darcy began the formal process of introducing the new mistress to each of those in the line, from the housekeeper Mrs.

Reynolds and the steward Mr. Lewis on down. She received and acknowledged courtesies with each of them, with a kind word to the youngest, most anxious of the bunch.

It was early in the afternoon, and the travelers were fatigued from their several days on the road. When Darcy led his wife into the house's grand foyer, she was as overwhelmed as she'd ever been—it was indeed superior to the great house at Rosings—and, seeing this, her husband insisted that she and Jane go to their rooms to recover.

And after an extended nap, Mrs. Darcy rose and rang, and Mrs. Reynolds appeared with a younger woman who would become Elizabeth's country maid. She was slightly above Elizabeth's age and had come from her family's leasehold farm some miles outside Lambton. Her name was Mary Alford, and she was shorter than Elizabeth and walked with a slight limp that was the result of childhood accident involving a horse.

Mrs. Reynolds had discussed with Darcy when the group arrived and they agreed that by temperament and ability Mary Alford was the ideal servant for Elizabeth—and time would prove this to be the case—and so on this first evening at Pemberley, Mrs. Reynolds left the mistress and her maid alone so the former could be prepared for dinner.

It was a fine dinner with just the two couples. Indeed, there was great familiarity, as the four supped together nearly every night when they were all in London that they'd stayed in, even before Darcy proposed.

The peace of the night was enchanting so they sat on a patio that took advantage of the eastern aspect of the house, where they could see the rising moon and marvel at the stars in the clear air and hear the various creatures who filled the Pemberley Woods.

And some hour after they sat, and after a contagion of poorly concealed yawns, the four rose. They climbed to their rooms, with Jane joining her sister in hers. Their maids assisted them but only briefly as the two Bennets (as they in some respects were no longer but in others would always be) were pleased to be left alone. Jane lay on Elizabeth's turned-down bed as Lizzy sat on its side.

"Could you have imagined this?"

"Oh, Jane. When we were such girls and assembled late at night quite like this at Longbourn. For so long, I could not allow myself to think that we'd be able to find love."

"And now?"

Lizzy looked down. "And now I will not allow myself to think that we can live without it."

"No, Mrs. Darcy, *we* cannot," Jane said with a great smile.

She wrestled herself up from the comfortable bed and to her feet. She dangled her hand towards Elizabeth. Her sister took it.

"And tonight, my dear, you will learn what living with love in all its wonderful aspects will mean."

She leaned down to give a kiss to her younger sister's forehead. Without a further word, she turned and left, gently closing the thick door behind her.

For a moment, and little more than that, Elizabeth Darcy was alone in her room at Pemberley.

THE END

Becoming Catherine Bennet

This is my second effort at a large work related to *Pride and Prejudice*. The first is *Becoming Catherine Bennet*, which is also on Kindle Unlimited as well as being available in paperback and hardcover. Here are the first two chapters of that novel, which accepts PandP except for allowing Kitty Bennet to head north to Newcastle to be with Lt. and Mrs. George Wickham. The first chapters can be found at:

https://dermodyhouse.com/books/becoming-catherine-bennet/

A Note About *Belinda*

In Chapter 25, there is a reference to Maria Edgeworth's novel *Belinda*. It occurs when Elizabeth and Margaret visit Mr. Johnson's bookshop on Bond Street:

> *For a select few of his lady patrons, [Mr. Johnson] procured copies of an early edition of* Belinda. *Elizabeth and Margaret were among those allowed to share a copy of that version of Miss Edgeworth's book.*

In *Jane Austen, the Secret Radical*, Helena Kelly writes that *Belinda* is referred to early in *Northanger Abbey*, where Miss Austen discusses the development of more series books—"novels"—growing in popularity and particularly at odds with the trend of gothic books that form the heart of Catherine Morland's reading (a trend referred to in this novella). This is from Chapter 5 of *Northanger*:

> *"I am no novel-reader—I seldom look into novels—Do not imagine that I often read novels—It is really very well for a novel." Such is the common cant. "And what are you reading, Miss—?" "Oh! It is only a novel!" replies the young lady, while she lays down her book with affected indifference, or momentary shame. "It is only* Cecilia, *or* Camilla, *or* Belinda"; *or, in short, only some work in which the greatest powers of the mind are displayed, in which the most thorough knowledge of human nature, the happiest delineation of its varieties, the liveliest effusions of wit and humour, are conveyed to the world in the best-chosen language.*

Alas, to Miss Austen, it seems that a reader would be embarrassed being seen with a "novel." Kelly asserts that though Northanger was published after Miss Austen's death, it was barely changed when published from its original form. This raises the following matter, to which this novella's reference to an early edition of *Belinda* is directed. It is that the first edition, as Kelly notes (I have not read it):

One of the books [referred to in Northanger*] that had "undergone considerable changes" between 1803 and 1816 was Maria Edgeworth's* Belinda. *In the original version of the novel readers would have found reference to an interracial marriage. They would also have found a heroine who gives serious consideration to marrying a "Creole" character....The 1810 edition of the novel, though, excises every suggestion of interracial or possibly interracial relationships. [*Secret Radical, *at 43-44.]*

Some Supplemental Material

Dear Miss Bennet

In writing this, I did a slight side-project: What if Wickham wrote to Elizabeth about Darcy's accusations? This applies to *Pride and Prejudice* itself.

I created a letter along those lines, and much of the contents of this letter are as George Wickham spoke them to Elizabeth.

INTRODUCTION

Cambridge
June 14, 1914

It has long been speculated that the noted mid-19th Century clergyman and philanthropist William Collins, Jr. had a family relationship with Catherine Bennet, with whom he did much of his work related to charities for the protection of pregnant, unmarried maids.

Recently, materials from Pemberley, the home of Catherine Bennet's sister Elizabeth Darcy, have become available to scholars for the first time. They reveal numerous things about the family.

One of the more interesting is a letter sent in 1812 from George Wickham to Elizabeth Bennet (as she then was). Wickham married another of Elizabeth Darcy's sisters, Lydia Wickham. Mr. and Mrs. George Wickham both died young. He at Waterloo in June 1815, and she while giving birth to a daughter, Lydia Denny. Mr. and Mrs. Wickham had one child, a boy named George Wickham, Jr., who, of course, is duly appreciated as an artist of the first degree. (A Mr. Denny is mentioned in this letter and I believe it likely that he became the widow Lydia Wickham's second husband. The history of that daughter is lost.)

George Wickham, Jr. was raised chiefly by his mother's sister Jane and Jane's husband Charles Bingley. In the course of researching Mr. and Mrs. Bingley, much was learned about another of his mother's sisters, Mrs. Elizabeth Darcy, as was Bennet. While the Darcys had several children, their affairs are also lost to history beyond Mr. Darcy's son and grandson residing at the family estate known as Pemberley, in Derbyshire County.

Mr. Darcy's only sibling, a much younger sister named Georgiana, did emerge with Catherine Bennet and Georgiana Darcy's cousin Anne de Bourgh, of Rosings in Kent (whose mother Lady Catherine de Bourg is mentioned in this letter), as a moving figure in the charity first mentioned. She was married to Edward Evans, an MP from County Wexford in Ireland, and they had several children about whom little is known.

In the course of my research, I came upon an interesting letter that suggests an intersection among numerous strands of these families. As it was written over a century ago, I feel no hesitancy in publishing it to the world to provide some new information concerning the family. This particular communication was found mixed among items of woman's clothing that were recovered from a trunk long stored in an attic at Pemberley. It was only recently that the trunk was opened. This communiction was found to be in remarkable condition, though it is over a century old, and appears to have spent virtually the entirety of that period protected where it was found.

Here are its contents.

J.W.

*　*　*　*

DATE, 1812

My Dear Miss Elizabeth,

Please do not be shocked upon your receipt of this lengthy communication. I ask that you not advise others immediately—though I frame this only as a request—of it or its contents. I assure you that I expect that efforts are being undertaken to locate me and your sweet, innocent sister Lydia but nothing in this will provide a morsel of information of where we are. I assure you that she is safe and maintains her virtue with me and in a way is under my protection in London, but I cannot reveal myself or our whereabouts until I have resolved a number of pressing matters that weigh heavily on me.

I make no excuse for what I have done. It was imprudent and more importantly wrong as to your sister. For reasons I hope to explain to you—I know that no explanation could be satisfactory—I took advantage of her girlish fascination with us officers and allowed my vanity to overcome my integrity.

I can, I believe, in time love her but in any case am obligated to do what I can to ensure her happiness.

Now to the matters at hand.

It came to my attention that while you were in Kent recently you received some sort of letter from Fitzwilliam Darcy and that this letter impugned my character. Upon receipt of that, I regret that you made no effort to communicate with me as to the truth of what he said concerning me. Your failure, Miss Elizabeth, was painful indeed and I stewed over it and stewed over it until it burst into the misconduct that has put me, and sweet Lydia, in our current positions. Again, I do not attempt to justify any of my recent behaviour. It is, as I say, my attempt at explaining my actions.

I have not of course seen Mr. Darcy's letter, but as it concerns me, I can imagine what he said and I can imagine that there are two matters about which he maligned me. These are my being denied the living that his father promised me and how I supposedly wronged his sister and charge, Georgiana.

I will address the first. During our many pleasant conversations, you will recall that I spoke of Mr. Darcy having deprived me of the living. I did, in fact, speak with him after his father's death concerning it. The living was occupied and no one knew for how long. His father left me a legacy of one thousand pounds but it would be some time until the living would be mine.

I will confess that I felt some attractions to town and being the son of a steward who'd begun as a lawyer before dedicating himself to the late Mr. Darcy and a graduate of Cambridge—paid for generously by the late Mr. Darcy himself—I thought I might venture into the law as a good profession and that I would do so in London.

In the combination of these things, I asked Darcy whether he would pay me the value of the living, which he did. He provided me with three thousand pounds. Alas, I found the temptations of London too much for a man who grew up somewhat wild on the grounds of Pemberley and I fell into a life of some gambling and debauchery and drink. I will admit it. I am sure Darcy has proclaimed it to be true and in this he is absolutely correct.

After several years, I learned that the incumbent of the living had died. I thought the availability of it would afford me the opportunity to turn to a life I felt better suited for than I found the law in London to be. I was, I admit, in quite a bad way but expected that he, given our long acquaintance—I once thought it might have been a friendship but realize that was not the case with him—and his quite ample financial reserves, would at least give a fair consideration of my entreaty.

Alas, he rejected it the several times I made it and I was forced to return to town to fend for myself. I still had sufficient influence in my small world and was able to maintain myself by acting in strict accordance with the restrictions I realized I needed to abide by. Indeed, Miss Elizabeth, I knew I had no choice in the matter.

I have often wondered what would have become of me had I either taken the living when the younger Mr. Darcy was ready to comply with the wishes of his father, which I so foolishly, in looking back at it, exchanged for "pieces of silver," or had he been willing to afford me a second opportunity to have it when he knew how desperately I was for it.

This is all as I told you when we had so many pleasant conversations in Meryton. As you saw then, I had sufficiently accepted that the law was not the profession for me and I had the good fortune of meeting my friend, Mr. Denny (who I hope you recall with fondness as he does you) who obtained a position for me as an officer in the militia that was boarding in Meryton. It was there that I had the good fortune of becoming acquainted with you and your lovely family (which I hope that you recall with some fondness, too).

I am sure that Mr. Darcy had his reasons for insisting on refusing my plea for the living. He does not, I know, easily find himself offering others a second chance, and I suppose he has money and position enough for him to do so.

It was his right. It was a living that he controlled to do with as he pleased. If I gave you the impression that he did not offer it to me and that he therefore violated the plain wishes of his much-loved father I apologize but the scars from his later denying it to me were perhaps too fresh for me to clarify that.

I will not label him a dishonourable man for that. I will say that to me at least he is an unnecessarily harsh one.

I assume as well that he wrote to you about my dealings with his dear sister Georgiana. I assure you that I do think her a dear creature, though at times too influenced by her brother's pride and haughtiness.

I will begin with Mrs. Younge. I assume his tale makes reference to her being some sort of evil co-conspirator as to his sister. To the contrary, I assure you that she is a good woman. I met her some years ago. Her husband had died six months before and she told me that he was a cruel man who'd squandered the money she brought to the marriage and turned to alcohol and died in a most undignified manner, specifically by drowning in a ditch into which he fell between the tavern he frequented and the home he ruled over.

I was quite young and had come to know Mrs. Younge on a casual basis since she often sat at the front of her house, which stood on the main road between Lambton and Pemberley. I will admit that I comforted her and that in my youth and in her gratitude for being freed of the onus of her horrible husband we did share a bed on many occasions. I will not deny that I took pleasure in what I was doing, as I believe she did as well.

She could not live long in the house and returned to Yorkshire whence she'd come and I heard no more of her for many years. We happened upon each other in far more pleasing circumstances in London, where I had gone to pursue my legal studies which, as I have said, did not take.

She was a far more assured woman than she had been when I'd last seen her in Derbyshire and I was exceedingly pleased with her. I confess that I may have had some feelings towards her and might have pursued them had she not laughed at what we had done as the "silliness of the young."

She assured me that she had found herself quite content as a widow and had used the education she received in her youth to obtain several positions as a governess and that, as it happened, she had been retained by Mr. Darcy and his cousin Colonel Fitzwilliam to act as Miss Darcy's governess.

I knew Miss Darcy quite well. You have of course met Mr. Darcy and he is ten years her senior. With their mother (and Lady Catherine de Bourgh's sister) Lady Anne Darcy sadly dead, Georgiana was in need of support and when she was not away at school, I often humoured her and I believe she was fond of me nearly as a brother since Darcy himself quite naturally fell into the role of a sort of father to her.

To be clear, Miss Elizabeth, I do not for one moment question how Darcy dealt with his sister. In family matters, he is a good, kind, and considerate man. I can vouch for the same characteristics with respect to those who worked at Pemberley, including my dear father. I have seen this time and time again. Again I realize I may have said otherwise when I first met you, but my sentiments at that time about Mr. Darcy were not as they should have been.

I must also vouch for the fact that I was not always as good, kind, and considerate to those around me, though I believe I have aged from those unadmirable traits, as I believe you yourself have witnessed.

As I said, when I met Mrs. Younge in town, Georgiana was her charge and I was quite pleased for them both, knowing them both to be of a good quality. I assure you, Miss Elizabeth, that notwithstanding her liaisons with me in the desperate period of her life, Mrs. Younge is among the most moral people with whom

I have had the good fortune to have met. (I assure you that I believe you to be of that calibre as well.)

I believe that Mrs. Younge must have told Georgiana that she met me near Temple Bar because some days later, Mrs. Younge sat on a bench close to where our first encounter occurred. I was exceedingly surprised to see her but in no means upset. She was a good friend to me who I had neglected for too long and I harboured the notion of resuming appropriate contact with her. I did not by then have any manly feelings towards her and I am certain she had no womanly ones regarding me.

When she rose to speak to me that day, she seemed quite upset. Though I do not recall the precise words, I promise that these were the sentiments expressed.

Mrs. Younge told me that Georgiana brightened up immediately on the mere mention of my name. Her brother did not visit as often as she would like and she quite missed being at Pemberley. How she would enjoy going for long walks in the Pemberley Woods. Those woods were where, Miss Elizabeth, Darcy and I spent countless hours as children and young lads and I too often miss them even these many years since. Perhaps you will some day have the opportunity to visit them yourself and will experience the magic that they have.

Georgiana often went for long walks in Hyde Park with her governess but being alone in London seemed far more repressive than in Derbyshire since there she would not encounter a person unaffiliated with the house for days on end and in town she saw dozens of such each block, each oblivious to the other.

I believe she must have obtained ideas from some of the books she read while alone, of ladies being carried away by a saviour from whatever drudgery their lives were. I met with her and Mrs. Younge as we arranged. Mrs. Younge told me that it seemed that until Georgiana saw and spoke with me, the fever concerning me—if I may be modest for a moment, however undeserved that fever was—would not break.

She was still very much a girl who had expectations of more than the indulgences I directed her way when she was even more of one. She was, I admit, on the cusp of becoming a woman and in a first flowering of what I believe will turn out to be a great beauty.

I was, I promise you, quite oblivious to this in any but a brotherly way. I had known her for many years and it would have been wildly inappropriate for me to treat her otherwise.

I immediately saw when we met, however, that those notions she'd picked up in her stories had become deeply set in for her. She insisted that I run off with her. She insisted that she would not survive were I not to do so.

I told her how inappropriate it was, that her feelings, such as they were, were wildly misplaced and that she needed to mature, that she should not have any serious thoughts in that way at least until she'd come out.

She was ignorant to what I said and to what Mrs. Younge said she told her. Mrs. Younge knew her as a quite compliant student and was surprised at the vehemence of her emotional outburst directed at me. It was perhaps, I think, not *me* in particular that she directed them but to the presence of any man with whom she'd long felt comfortable. I was to be her knight-in-signing-armour, you see.

It happened that Mrs. Younge had arranged—as Darcy full knew—to take Georgiana for a fortnight's stay in Ramsgate. Her initial hope was that her separation from me would break the fever, but a day or two after they arrived she wrote back to me, explaining that if anything Georgiana's obsession, for that's what it had become, had gotten worse. "We must do something," she said, and I arrived the very next morning. We met along the sea wall and she was upon me immediately, such that many observers looked and I believe assumed that we were brother and sister.

Mrs. Younge told me that the only way that we could rid Georgiana of her delusions and fantasies so that she could assume the proper growth into a woman—forgive me for presuming to know such things but I have thought long on it and believe it may be at least in some respects accurate—was to engage with a charade.

In desperation, Mrs. Younge suggested that we enroll her brother in our scheme. I know you are shocked to hear me say that, but it is the truth. The only way to convince Georgiana of the folly of our actually marrying was to make her believe that I shared her desires in this way, knowing that her brother would not allow it. This was for many reasons, not least because of her young age and vulnerability of spirit.

So after we met by the sea wall, we walked to a tavern near the water. I said that I would marry her. I know I should not have said any such thing, but I saw no alternative. She asked me when and begged that I take her to Scotland so we could be "husband and wife" immediately.

I told her that such a step would not do. That we would forever be exiled unless we married properly, in an English church with her brother's consent.

As I said, I knew her brother would never consent and that would be the end of it. Before this plan could be achieved, however, Darcy appeared. He confronted me and Mrs. Younge but would not hear us. You can imagine how livid he was. He is a man, as I believe we both know, of a taciturn manner but when his emotions are brought to a boil they do not simmer but explode.

Knowing that his anger at me and Mrs. Younge would result in causing his sister to rebel against us and not against him—as she truly is in awe of him and would never do anything that he was adamantly against—we abandoned Ramsgate.

I very much regret depriving Mrs. Younge of what was a fine position as governess and have not had the opportunity of communicating with her since. But insofar as any aspersions are made as to her, indeed as to the entirety of her character, I assure you they are misplaced. She is a fine, considerate, and educated woman who did not deserve such censure as Darcy likely imposed on her.

I never saw Georgiana again. As you have yourself witnessed, I have never had the opportunity to speak to her brother about her and I hope that she is blooming into the fine woman I expect her to become. If you do happen upon her, I ask that you not mention me for I fear it will rekindle memories of a very awkward time for her, a time I fear has been wildly misinterpreted by several, including Mr. Darcy.

In this, I do not blame Darcy. He was, as always, acting in what he perceived to be the best interests of his dear sister. And I assure you that she is a dear sister to him and was nearly one to me. I regret certain of my later dealings with her in Ramsgate, but I promise you that they were done in good faith and in the honest opinion that they were in her best interests.

I do not blame Darcy for what he said about me in this regard. To him, it had all the appearances of me attempting, with the help of Mrs. Younge, to elope with Georgiana to revenge myself on him and snare her fortune, which I admit to knowing was considerable. In this, as I have shown, he was mistaken in the conclusions that he doubtless reached.

* * * *

Your sister sits near me as I write this. I know that you will conclude from her presence and the circumstances that have led her to be here belie my claims of innocence regarding Georgiana Darcy. I give you my word as a gentleman, however, that what I have written is the truth. I hope that while you may never forgive me for what I have done with Lydia—though I hope our marriage will establish itself as a good and happy one—you will not consider me to have acted improperly with regard to whatever Mr. Darcy has said about me.

As to Lydia, who is a sweet girl also on the verge of becoming a woman, I fear that unlike with Georgiana Darcy I acted impulsively and, I cannot say it often enough, wrongly. She is my beautiful cross to bear, but I carry it willingly and hope that in the years to come I establish myself as the good and faithful and doting husband that she—as well as at least one other of the Bennet girls—deserve.

I am,
&c, &c,
George Wickham

Acknowledgements

I have the generous support of several pre-publication readers who contributed mightily to the final product, although I bear responsibility for the defects with it.

I was fortunate to have a number of people help me as beta readers, for whom I am grateful: Melissa Anne Barbato, Renée Gendron, Liz Hart, Lisa Manion, Harriet Miller, and Leah Pruett.

The Author

Joseph P. Garland has written numerous stories and several novels. This is his first venture into the world of Jane Austen. He has published three novels set in the early years of the Gilded Age in New York and a contemporary novel set chiefly in New York. He is a New York lawyer.

His books can be found at:
https://dermodyhouse.com/books/

Pride and Prejudice Sequel

Becoming Catherine Bennet

Gilded Age

Róisín Campbell: An Irishwoman in New York
A Studio on Bleecker Street
A Maid's Life

Contemporary

I Am Alex Locus: My Search for the Truth

Printed in Great Britain
by Amazon